W9-BKL-733

YOUNG ZORRO

THE IRON BRAND

YOUNG ZORRO

THE IRON BRAND

by DIEGO VEGA,
a descendant of Zorro,
as told to JAN ADKINS
Based on the novel ZORRO *by Isabel Allende*

rayo

HARPERCOLLINS*PUBLISHERS*

Rayo is an imprint of HarperCollins Publishers Inc.

Young Zorro: The Iron Brand

Copyright © 2006 by Zorro Productions, Inc.

Library of Congress Cataloging-in-Publication Data is available.
ISBN-10: 0-06-083945-7 — ISBN-10: 0-06-083946-5 (lib. bdg.)
ISBN-13: 978-0-06-083945-1 — ISBN-13: 978-0-06-083946-8 (lib. bdg.)
Typography by Hilary Zarycky
1 2 3 4 5 6 7 8 9 10
❖
First Edition

THE IRON BRAND

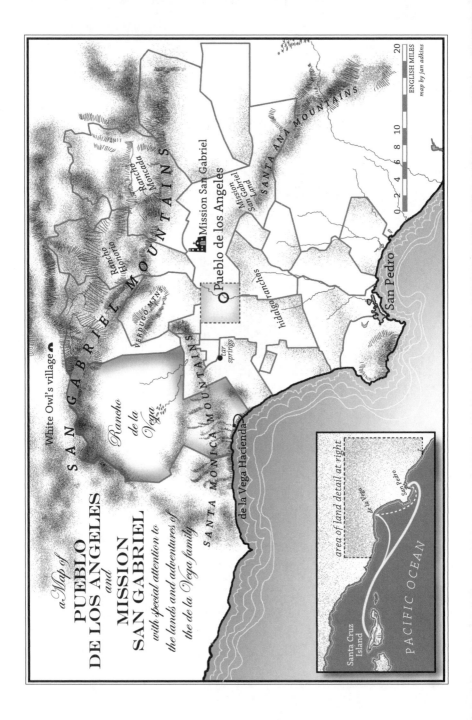

a Map of
**PUEBLO
DE LOS ANGELES**
and
**MISSION
SAN GABRIEL**

*with special attention to
the lands and adventures of
the de la Vega family*

White Owl's village

Rancho
Moncada

Rancho
Honorio

VERDUGO MTNS

SAN GABRIEL MOUNTAINS

Rancho
de la Vega

tar
springs

Mission San Gabriel

Pueblo de los Angeles

Mission
San Gabriel
San Land

hidalgo ranchos

SANTA MONICA MOUNTAINS

SANTA ANA MOUNTAINS

de la Vega Hacienda

San Pedro

0 2 4 6 8 10   20
ENGLISH MILES
map by jan adkins

area of land detail at right

de la Vega

San Pedro

Santa Cruz Island

PACIFIC OCEAN

—〜 1 〜—

TWO MYSTERIES

PACO PEDERNALES WAS PLEASED with himself. He had the tired and happy feeling of finishing a good job. He was a fine carpenter, trained by the padres of the San Gabriel Mission, and he had just built a wall of bookshelves and cabinets in the lavish hacienda of Don Miguel Moncada. He had coins in his pocket and knew his wife had a good meal waiting for him.

This was a Thursday evening in late March, in the year 1810, near the Pueblo de los Angeles. Paco's burro was patiently carrying his boxes of tools. He spoke to it now and then: "Soon, Maria, soon. I'll take those heavy boxes from your back and you can eat hay while I eat tamales, yes? You're a good friend. We'll be home soon."

He reached a place where the road dipped into a streambed. The light was dim. As he looked hard to find the stepping-stones across the stream, a voice called, "Paco!"

He turned, smiling. This was a pleasant surprise: he would have the company of a friend on his walk to the pueblo.

A hard leather loop fell around his shoulders and tightened painfully, binding his arms to his sides. A gag was pushed into his mouth, and a rag tied around his eyes. In a few seconds his hands were bound with leather strips. A deep, hard voice said, "Welcome, brother carpenter. You're coming on a trip with us. Aren't you lucky?"

A sudden blow to the side of his head convinced Paco that he was not so lucky. The meal his wife had cooked would grow cold, and then she would wonder what became of her husband. It would be a mystery.

Almost two hundred years after Paco Pedernales disappeared, a small earthquake opened a secret room under an old hacienda in Los Angeles. On the walls of the room were whips, pistols, and a rack of wickedly thin swords. Hanging beside the swords were a black hat, a black cape, and a black mask. It was the secret den of el

Zorro, the legendary hero of Old California. There was also an iron-bound chest filled with papers.

In those papers were stories written by el Zorro himself, Don Diego de la Vega, or by his best friend and silent brother, Bernardo. Each of the objects with the papers—ornate candlesticks, lace shawls, maps, spurs—seemed to be part of a story.

The historians who sorted the papers tracked down the last of the de la Vegas—me. I learned that el Zorro was my ancestor.

In that treasure trove of stories I read all the wild and brave tales of el Zorro, that black-masked hero, a fighter for justice and defender of the weak. But the best stories were the tales of Diego and Bernardo when they were young—how they grew up on the vast de la Vega rancho and in the Gabrieleño Indian villages, the tricks they played and the mischief they made. This was before Diego became the real el Zorro, when he and Bernardo were just cub foxes. They were only boys in the stories, but justice meant so much to them, even then.

The first story was linked to one of those objects in the chest: a strange branding iron. It explained why Paco Pedernales was kidnapped on his walk home, long ago.

~⚬ 2 ⚬~

MOUNTAIN AND OCEAN

"DIEGO! DIEGO! GET UP, you sleepy boy!"

Bernardo was up and about. Estafina had seen him in the kitchen. As soon as that boy's eyes opened, he was out of his cot and headed for food.

Estafina swept through the boys' room and onto the sleeping porch. Was it possible Diego was up already and out the door?

It was curious about Diego and Bernardo. They should have been like two quail chicks, exactly the same. They'd been raised together all their lives.

"There you are, blanket pig!" Estafina saw Diego shifting beneath the covers.

Both were loose-limbed, awkward boys a few months shy of fifteen years old. They both ate like starved wolves. But beyond this—and a disgusting delight at noisy burping after meals—they were completely different.

"Dreamtime is over, Diego!" If he didn't jump out of bed, she would dust his bottom off with her long-handled broom.

Entirely different, and it wasn't just that Bernardo didn't speak. To tell the truth, Diego talked plenty for both of them. He was chatty enough to be annoying. He was the kind of boy grandmothers want to reach across the dinner table and rap with a spoon: "Hush!" Bernardo was calm, even somber at times.

Diego was tall and thin, all arms and legs connected loosely to a head that sprouted large ears. Bernardo was short and compact, sure-footed, and almost too careful. He had that strange ability to disappear in a room just by being still. Both were good runners and climbers, but Bernardo could move like a shadow, slipping from place to place without seeming to be anywhere between. People always saw Diego, and they mostly missed Bernardo.

"Get up, Diego! You can't sleep the day away!"

More than once Diego had been dragged from the big hall of the hacienda by a furious Estafina, twisting his ear and shouting, "Barnyard animal in the house! Out of here with your dung-caked sandals! Go foul the

7

house of the chickens!" While Bernardo, with sandals just as dirty, would slip out the other door, unnoticed. Diego longed to be invisible.

Tall and small, loud and quiet. Visible and invisible, excitable and calm. Morning wren and night owl. They were like reverse images of each other. Yet that's the way they lived, too, like images in a mirror. If you saw one, the other was nearby.

"Sleep is for the night; day is for work!" Estafina believed this so passionately that she tore the bedcovers off in a single heave.

"Aaah!" she bellowed. The goat named Flower looked up from Diego's bed, annoyed to be disturbed and then yelled at. She rose daintily to her feet and stepped down from the bed. She refused to stay in a place where she wasn't wanted.

Estafina swatted at the goat. Flower decided to leave more quickly. Estafina pursued it, yelling, "That boy is the devil's cousin!"

Diego looked out from the big wardrobe cupboard in which he had been hiding, stifling his laughter. As energetic as he was, he was not above wanting a few extra minutes of sleep in the morning. His prank had gone well, but now that he thought about it, a little breakfast might be good.

Mornings at the hacienda were full of light, songs from the caged birds, and the *pat-pat-pat* of someone making tortillas. There were all the pleasant noises of a great house preparing itself for the day—sweeping, water splashing on stone floors, the snap of sheets and blankets being shaken out of bedroom windows.

Diego climbed out of the wooden cupboard and washed his face in a basin. He dried himself with a coarse towel. He could smell tortillas on the griddle.

Horses nickered in the stable, a blacksmith was beating rhythm on a horseshoe and his anvil, someone was singing upstairs, and Bernardo was playing his flute back beyond the herb garden wall. The Santa Monica Mountains were brown and gold through the window; a breeze from the northwest brought the smell of the Pacific Ocean through the hacienda. Why would anyone live anyplace but the golden hills of California?

Diego came into the kitchen with a smile. "Estafina," he said, "you are so beautiful that everything for the rest of the day will look like mud." And he snatched up a fresh, hot tortilla.

Estafina snorted and aimed a halfhearted swing of her broom at him. "Diego the goat boy! Take a tortilla for Bernardo, too. Regina wants both of you in her sitting room."

Sometimes Estafina and Regina called each other by name. They were both Gabrieleño Indians of the same tribe. When they were arguing, Estafina called Regina "Mistress" and Regina called Estafina "Señora Esposito." With Mistress Regina, there were many arguments. Padre Mendoza, always diplomatic, described Regina de la Vega as a woman of "high spirits." This was a hot pepper of caution wrapped in a tortilla of praise. She could be warm and charming. She could also lash out with a tongue so sharp that it took the skin off your hopes.

It wasn't surprising that she was fiery. She had not been raised to be the mild and mannerly mistress of a hacienda. As a young woman, her name was Toypurnia. She was a ruthless and deadly warrior, and her fierce warrior heart was never far beneath the polite surface.

The only way Diego could ever make sense of his parents' stormy, up-and-down marriage was that they had met at sword point. Captain Alejandro de la Vega had fought off an Indian raid on the Pueblo de los Angeles led by the war chief Toypurnia. He had killed many raiders and wounded their leader. Only when the battle was over did the captain discover the lean and lovely face of a young goddess. Of course he fell in love with her. How could their marriage be anything but stormy?

But today Regina looked up from her household account books with affection. "You boys are growing up," she said, smiling. "Look at these handsome young *Californios*. Too soon the hacienda will be howling and wailing with the sound of your babies."

"*Mamá!*" Diego blushed and scowled at her teasing, but Bernardo only shook his head.

Regina reached out and smoothed Bernardo's hair. "Your dear mother would be proud of her son," she said. His mother had been her best friend. The two women had given birth to the boys within days of each other. When Regina was wracked with a fever after the birth, Bernardo's mother had nursed both boys. This was why they were called "milk brothers," and they had a special bond. As a very young child, Bernardo had seen his mother murdered by pirate raiders. Since that dark day, the boy had never spoken. Of course Regina had raised him as her own. Bernardo was a part of the family, a member of the household, though Don Alejandro could never quite let go of the class distinction between them as *patrón* and Indian, Spanish conqueror and native.

"Now there's work to do," she said. "I've had our good potter, Señor Porcana, make some bowls and serving plates for me. And some mugs to replace the dozens that are broken." She gave the boys a sharp glance from under her eyebrows. "So you will please me by riding into the pueblo with packhorses and picking up the pottery. I have some notes for the padre, some gifts for the good brothers, and if any ships have arrived you may fetch the packages for us. Now, do you understand?"

"*Sí, Mamá*. And should we discover a mine of gold on the way, we'll become the richest young hidalgos in California."

"But while you are gathering your riches, you will be careful with my pottery," Regina said over a stern finger.

With the letters and packages for Padre Mendoza and his Franciscan brothers, she gave them a few coins. "Perhaps the baker at the pueblo has something to interest two brave young *Californios*. If you find the gold mine, you can pay me back. Be home by dark."

Out in the horse corrals, Diego slipped a halter over Lucrecia's long, mild face. She was an old friend, a big sand-colored mare, quiet but powerful. He knew she could lope across the grasslands all day long. Thick saddle blankets went over her broad back, then the wooden saddle. He tightened the saddle's bull-hide girth. He laid the soft leather *mochila* over the wooden saddle tree. Since this was the pad that rode between Diego's backside and the wood, he placed it carefully.

Bernardo walked into the barn with Frying Pan, an iron-gray mule, following him like a long-eared dog. Even without words he could charm the wildest horse and, with a few hand strokes or clicks of his tongue, calm a skittish mount.

"No, Bernardo, you're not taking a mule. We have the finest horses on the coast, and you ride around like a poor padre on a lop-eared mule! What's wrong with riding a real vaquero's horse?"

Bernardo ignored him, cinching up the saddle girth. He made a rude noise with his tongue. Frying Pan looked at Diego and seemed to grin, not caring what he thought.

"You and your mules. You're as stubborn as one!"

Mules or horses, they were careful riders. They had both learned from their idol, Scar, the rancho's managing *mayordomo*.

"You want to be a real rider?" he would say. "Something more than a grin strapped to a horse's back? Then ride with the horse. Ride *in* the horse." Scar had made them fine horsemen, even among *Californios*—and the fancy people in Mexico City joked that their *Californio* country cousins would walk two hundred paces to ride a horse fifty paces.

Lucrecia and Frying Pan waited patiently while Diego and Bernardo haltered four mules and cinched on the wooden packsaddles. Scar and horses had taught them patience.

"A real caballero takes his time," Scar said. "Horses hate these jump-up-and-ride-off jackrabbits. The horse remembers. It has a big heart that knows your heart. You ride like you love the horse, it will know. Take your time with every blanket and cinch. Love the horse's back like your own."

They were almost finished when Scar and their other idol rode into the stable yard.

"Hola, hijos," Don Alejandro called. "Hello, boys. Off to town for your mother?" Diego's father stepped off his stallion while it was still moving and snapped the reins over a hitching post. *Capitán* Alejandro de la Vega was as straight as a ramrod, like a soldier on parade. He wore the hidalgo's colorful, embroidered clothes with a red sash.

Scar wore the vaquero's old-fashioned short pants

over leggings. He slid down from the saddle soundlessly and loosened his horse's girth, then loosened the girth of his *patrón's* horse.

Both men jingled when they walked toward the house, the big rowels of their spurs spinning in the dust.

"Is all well, *Papá?*" Diego asked. His father's brow was creased.

"Well?" Don Alejandro stopped, frowned a moment, and replied, "All is never well on a rancho this size. Señor Pedernales, the carpenter, should have come yesterday, but he's nowhere to be found. Disappeared. And we're losing de la Vega cattle, boys. A few hundred head." This was a small part of the thousands of steers the rancho owned on the broad grazing lands of Pueblo de los Angeles. But Diego knew that cattle were the lifeblood of the pueblo and of the rancho. What does a rancher worry about? Cattle and water and cattle and feed and cattle.

"Could it be bears?"

"Not unless every bear is the size of the mission church."

"Indians from the mountains?"

Don Alejandro loosened his chin cord and took off his hat. "I doubt it." He looked at Diego and Bernardo with a little smile. "If you were an Indian, even from the far mountains, would you steal the cattle of White Owl's son-in-law? Perhaps they're braver than I am. Your grandmother is tougher than Scar, here. More dangerous, too."

Scar chuckled, a rare sound.

Bernardo's hands flashed from his stomach to his head in the sign for illness.

"Yes," Don Alejandro said. "That could be it. A cattle sickness. But we're not finding dead cattle. It's a mystery to me. Keep your eyes open, boys. So, you're going to the pueblo to fetch something?"

"*Sí, Papá.* We're picking up things at the potter's for *Mamá* and delivering letters to the padres. If a ship has come in, we'll pick up packages for the rancho."

"A good day's ride," Don Alejandro said. "Perhaps you will do me the service of stopping at the shop of Julio Dos Ochos. He may have a few branding irons ready for this year's *apartado.*" The parting of the herds into each rancho's share and the branding of new calves was one of the pueblo's most important times.

"*Sí, Papá.*"

"*Vayan con Dios, hijos,*" he said. "Go with God, boys." He strode into the house.

Scar walked among the pack animals, inspecting the

saddles and girths. He tightened one girth but said nothing, and this was high praise from the *mayordomo*.

As Scar jingled into the dark hacienda, the sound of loud, arguing voices rolled through the sitting room window. Don Alejandro and Regina were battling over some small thing. Bernardo put his fingers in his ears and squinted his eyes shut.

"Saints and cats and little fishes," Diego said. "Yes, let's get out of here."

They mounted up and started along the tree-lined trail toward the mountains. They rode a few hundred paces and stopped to retighten their girths. Diego looked back through the trees to the hacienda's garden. His mother and father were walking in the garden with their heads affectionately together.

"Remind me, Bernardo, never to marry. I will never understand how men and women go together."

Bernardo nodded, agreeing, and Frying Pan brayed.

~ 3 ~

THE PUEBLO

AFTER SEVERAL HOURS' RIDE across the plain, they were glad to see the buildings of the Pueblo de los Angeles.

It was a prosperous pueblo. It had several streets, a few real stores, dozens of houses, and the workshops of skilled craftspeople. It even had an inn. Out here on the edge of the world, Los Angeles was—at least to its settlers—a promising bud of civilization.

Friends called out from the porches and doorways of the thick-walled adobe buildings. Perhaps three hundred *Angeleños* lived around the pueblo. A few hundred lived out on the ranchos. Another four hundred neophytes, Indian workers who had converted to the Catholic church, lived near the mission. All told, only about a thousand souls, so there was no reason not to know everyone. Like many places on the edge of the world, it was friendly.

Diego and Bernardo tethered their animals in the shade of some oaks and walked toward the plaza. Bernardo tipped back his thumb and little finger in a drinking motion.

"Me too. I could do with some *agua fresca* after that ride."

They crossed the dusty road toward the trees and benches of the plaza. Suddenly a troop of horsemen thundered around a corner. They were dressed like vaqueros bound for a fiesta, but they were just boys, not much older than Diego and Bernardo. They were the young dandies of the pueblo, the idle sons of rich hidalgos looking for a scrap of excitement. Silver conchos winked from their saddles and hatbands. Their big-roweled spurs gleamed, and their quirts snapped at their horses' flanks. The leader of the band turned straight for the two boys in the street.

Both boys stood still, knowing that horses won't willingly ride over a basket, much less a person. With wild cries and cracking whips, the gang of boys galloped down on them. Bernardo grasped the hem of his loose shirt.

When the riders were only a few horse lengths away,

19

Bernardo gave a piercing whistle and pulled his shirt up, inside out, over his head. To the horses he appeared suddenly seven feet tall, white, and unfamiliar. The horses panicked, skidding to a halt. Some reared and stumbled, some slid and clambered. All but two of the riders were dismounted, thumping into the dust.

They picked themselves up, cursing. They were no longer imaginary dons and grand vaqueros; they were just dismounted boys slapping away the dust and dung from their embroidered costumes.

The leader, Rafael Moncada, older than the boys by five years, leaped up in a cloud of dust. "Fools! What do you mean by frightening our horses?" he demanded. "Someone could have been hurt. These horses are fine racing stock, not broken-down wagon pullers." He mounted and pointed to Bernardo. "Even an idiot Indian like this should know better."

The leader raised his quirt to lash Bernardo. Before he could bring it down, Bernardo ducked under his horse's belly and tapped its far-side jaw so it leaped sideways. One of the dandies howled with pain as a heavy hoof stamped on his fancy boot. At the same moment, Diego leaped at the leader, now hanging halfway out of the saddle. Though he was stockier and years older than Diego, the wiry boy jerked him down into the dust and pounded on him like a cat. No one could dare to whip Bernardo in front of Diego!

One of the leader's gang raised his own quirt, butt first, to club Diego. Bernardo toppled him into the dust as well. In the white cloud, boots clattered and bits of gravel flew. Another gang member saw his chance when Diego was on top of Moncada, pinning him: the sharp toe of a boot caught Diego in the ribs and rolled him to the side.

Diego breathed heavily, wincing in pain as Moncada stumbled to his feet.

"You insolent half-breed!" Moncada shouted, reaching clumsily for the sword hilt at his saddlebow.

But a voice, sounding as deep and powerful as the archangel Gabriel's, stopped him. "Señor Moncada! Take care for your immortal soul!"

The voice didn't come from the heavens, but from behind a fig tree in the plaza. Fray Feliipe Mendoza, leader of the mission friars, stepped out into the sunlight. "I think you have embarrassed yourself quite enough, young Moncada. You will have the sin of pride to confess before Sunday's mass. In another moment you might have burdened yourself with heavier sins. Give thanks, young Moncada, and go your way in peace."

Moncada seethed with frustration. He was about to say something to maintain his puffed-up dignity, but the padre was not in an indulgent mood. "Keep your tongue still, boy," he said quietly.

"And you," he said, pulling Diego and Bernardo to their feet with two powerful hands. "Fighting in the street like stray dogs. Shame!"

Mendoza turned to the others. "You've raised enough dust to make my teeth grit. Walk these horses out of the plaza and get back to your mothers. Tell them to wipe your noses. Go."

Moncada mounted and spurred his horse viciously. It leaped once, making some of his gang fall back, but he jerked the reins hard. The quivering horse stopped against the iron bit with a moan, its eyes crazy. Pulling his reins cruelly tight, Moncada rode away. The rest of them walked their horses away from the plaza, eager to be out of sight. The boy whose foot had been stepped on clung to his saddle for support, limping painfully.

Mendoza frowned and clucked his tongue at Diego and Bernardo, still holding them by the scruffs of their shirts. He let them go, pushing them toward the shade of the tavern's patio. He looked back after the retreating dandies and shook his head. "Young toughs. Proud Spanish blood." He laughed once. "They wouldn't have lasted long out here in the early days, back when your father was making this place safe, Diego." He almost growled, then brightened.

"Have you had enough excitement, then? Come, *hijos*, sit with me in the shade. The day grows warm, and we've had enough exercise. I'm working on a plate of beans and chiles that is much too big for me. Come help."

The padre sat down with a sigh. Only rarely did they remember that he was an old man, past sixty. Priests and monks might grow fat in Spain. But out here the padres taught their neophytes to ride and rope and brand, tan hides, plough, and build. The sun had burned Mendoza almost as brown as his robe. His fringe of white hair partly covered a missing ear from the battle in which Diego's mother led her people in an uprising against the Spanish. The padre was no soft psalm singer but was as tough as sandal leather.

"What brings you into the pueblo, *hijos*?"

"Partly you, Padre. My mother has sent you letters and gifts for your brothers."

"God bless Señora Regina. Sometimes"—he nodded his head toward the street where the gang of boys had made trouble—"sometimes I am tempted to despair. But we have been blessed in this place. Look," he said, pushing the plate of food toward them, "here are the beans and chiles. Grab a tortilla and bless yourselves."

He was right. It was too much food for one old padre. They rolled up fresh tortillas and scooped up the tangy beans and peppers. They drank mugs of *agua fresca*—cool water mixed with fruit juice and spices.

"Padre," Diego asked, "how can Rafael Moncada hate our Indian brothers? For him, the Indians who raise his crops and herd his cattle are no more than dogs."

Bernardo shook his head angrily.

The old monk turned a rolled tortilla in his fingers, examining it as if it had an answer. "Only God can look into our hearts. Rafael Moncada has his own demons that claw at his heart, making him hate. Hate is its own punishment, *hijos*." The old man dug into the beans and bit into his tortilla.

"Padre, have any ships come in recently?"

"Only a Boston merchant. No official ships have arrived for months. No mail, then, but there may be packages from Acapulco or Panama. If you mean to be back at the rancho by dark, you need to get along. I, too, must remount my mule and ride down toward the almond orchards. I am concerned that several of my farmers and tanners and carpenters are missing. It's curious because they are good, steady men. This morning Señora Pedernales came to me looking for Paco."

"*Sí*, Padre. My father asked about Señor Pedernales. How many are missing?"

"Perhaps a dozen, and they are all skilled men. In a little place like our pueblo, we need everyone's skills. I can't understand how or why they've dropped out of sight."

"We'll keep our eyes sharp. And, Padre, is the mission's herd missing any cattle?"

The old man looked up quickly. "My vaqueros tell me we've lost a few hundred head. I had passed it off as poor counting before the *apartado*, but why do you ask?"

"*Papá* tells me we are missing about the same number, but we don't know why. Bernardo thinks it may be a cattle sickness."

The monk shook his head. "I don't think so. We'd see sick cattle, and we'd find dead cattle. What evil things are happening in our pueblo?"

"I believe the Devil himself has stolen the people and the cattle to ask them, 'Who is this wise and holy Padre Mendoza?'"

"Ah, Diego, you have almost too much flattery in

you. You will go far. Probably as far as jail, but far." He grinned. *"Vayan con Dios, hijos."*

Diego and Bernardo picked up the new branding irons at the blacksmith shop: big de la Vega *V*s. The pottery shop was just down the street.

They watched from the doorway as Señor Porcana, a small man with big arms, sat at his pottery wheel. He kicked the heavy lower wheel around and around; the vertical shaft spun its upper wheel. He raised a head-sized lump of wet clay, then thumped it onto the spinning center with a loud "Ha!"

His hands held it steady, and the boys could see his thick forearms straining. The hair on his hands and arms was spattered and clotted with clay. His eyes were focused on the whirling mass. His thumping leg kept the wheel spinning. He dipped his hands into a bowl of water. When he touched them to the clay, it gleamed wetly. He leaned into the clay, one hand plunging into the center, one holding the outside. The hands worked against each other, drawing the brown clay up and around. It was like magic: a perfect shape appeared out of plain wet mud. It was as if the shape had always been there, waiting for him.

The wheel slowed. He plucked a wooden tool from

a rack beside the wheel and touched it to the soft clay once, twice, again. It made parallel lines on the pot's outside. Now he picked up a piece of string. He tossed a loop over the spinning pot, let it settle around the base, and pulled it straight. In a blink the string cut through the soft clay. He dropped the string and, before the pot could wobble, he lifted it in his fingertips.

Diego clapped, applauding his skill.

"Humph!" Señor Porcana said, responding to the compliment. "Any good potter could make this pot. Maybe not as well"—he held it up and turned it this way and that—"but it would probably hold cornmeal."

"Señor," Diego began.

As Porcana stepped down from the wheel carrying the pot, he interrupted Diego with a list: "Six large plates with acorn decorations, six dessert plates, same. Six big bowls and six little bowls. Also ten mugs. Who's breaking all the mugs in your hacienda? Three platters, big enough for roast piglet. Or a small boy, roasted." He squinted at the boys as if he were measuring them for a platter. Too big, he decided.

"Packed in straw and wood chips. Wrapped in sacking. By the back door. Ready to be carried away. And carefully!" he said, frowning back at them as he perched his fresh pot on a drying shelf. "You see that pile of ruined pots? You know what they're for?"

The boys shook their heads no.

"They're for throwing at boys who break my pots by galloping around with them! No broken pots! They leave here perfect; they arrive perfect. Now pack up and off with you! I've got too much to do, and I'm in a bad mood!"

The packages had odd shapes, some big, some small. They tied them to the wooden packsaddles, weaving a web of cords until they were secure.

When they were half a mile from the pueblo, Diego wondered aloud, "How could we tell if he was in a bad mood? He's always in a bad mood." As if reading Bernardo's mind, he added, "Yes, he's an artist. Yes, he does beautiful work. But why must he be so crusty? Perhaps his mother was bitten by a dog. Now he barks."

4

THE HARBOR

THEY RODE INTO THE cheerful mess that sur-
rounds every dock—stacks of lumber, ruined
barrels, abandoned anchors, wrecked boat
hulls, odd ends of rope, and plain trash.

Their mounts were tired and hot. They tied them in
the shade and fetched pails of water from a stream.

Thump, thump, thump. Matthew Stackpole came
stumping along the dock on his peg leg. "I thought I
saw you riding in." Matthew was from Boston and,
though he spoke Spanish, his accent was horrible.

"*Hola, Capitán* Stackpole," Diego greeted him. "I
trust the day smiles on you?"

"Not so bad as being hit with a log on the head," he
said. "And with you?"

"With us the day is like a lark singing. We are content.

What boat is in the harbor?"

"A boat from my home, Boston. The *Two Brothers*. I know the captain. A good sailor, even though he's a Nantucket man."

The boys didn't know what a Nantucket man was. It sounded awful.

"I've asked him in to visit, just to hear the Boston in him. Come sit and share a biscuit."

They walked out along the dock with him. Stackpole had one good leg and one whalebone leg. He'd been left on shore years ago by a whaling ship after a shark took off his leg at the knee.

United States vessels called at San Pedro occasionally. It was officially illegal to trade with non-Spanish vessels, but here on the edge of the world, rules were sometimes overlooked. Stackpole had become a kind of harbormaster. He sold marine supplies, made small boats, and repaired local fishing boats. He wasn't exactly part of the pueblo, because he wasn't a member of the church. Apparently people from Boston had their own kind of church and were particular about it. People from Boston were, the boys had learned, particular about nearly everything.

"Where's that pest Trinidad?" Diego asked. It was obvious, despite his words, that he liked her.

Stackpole waved out toward the water. "Yes, my pet mermaid sailed out to the *Two Brothers*. She'll be back in and complaining soon."

Stackpole opened a tin of biscuits and poured some tea into tin cups.

Trinidad Somoza was a half-wild homeless girl a bit younger than the boys. She lived in a shack near the boat shed, and Stackpole watched after her as well as he could. He made sure she ate and found her warm clothes when the weather turned.

He pointed with a biscuit to the little boat just leaving the *Two Brothers*. "She meets every boat coming in," he said, sighing, "and she asks if there's a message from her mother. Not much of a mother, really. I hear she lives in a fancy house in Acapulco. She sends a bit of money sometimes. Never writes. But Trinidad always thinks her mother is coming soon."

Bernardo remembered his mother's face and her arms around him. He was angry with a mother who stayed in Acapulco.

The little boat's sail rose, flapping at first. Then it perked up tight and filled with wind. The boat turned and surged over the water. They could hear the smack of its flat bottom against the waves.

Then they could see Trinidad at the tiller. Her head

31

bobbed up and down—up at the sail, forward at her course—totally focused on making the boat go. If Diego and Bernardo were half horse, she was half boat.

Clinging to the mast of the boat was a man in a blue uniform and cap. He looked nervous as Trinidad threaded her boat through buoys and pilings and other boats. Her red, frizzy hair was streaming back, and her teeth were white in her tanned, freckled face. She was one of those chirpy, tough little girls you had to like.

It looked like she was about to plow into the beach, but she freed the mainsheet, the line that controlled the sail. The sail swung out, and she spun the boat around. It stopped a handsbreadth from the floating dock. She leaped out and tied its docklines. Trinidad jumped aboard over her passenger and lowered the flapping sail into a quick, expert bundle. She was running up the slanting gangway while the Nantucket man was shakily climbing out of the boat.

"Bernardo! Diego!" She slapped the boys on their shoulders and threw herself onto the bench, seizing a tin cup. She poured herself tea and laced it with molasses. Bernardo made a sour face: molasses in tea?

"What's wrong with you, sourpuss? It's sweet and good for you. You could use a little sweetening up, Bernie."

Bernardo frowned. He hated her breezy nickname for him.

"Diego! How are things up on the rancho? When are you two coming to dive for some abalone with me? What have you got on all those packsaddles? Are you looking for packages for the rancho? Captain Carter has two for you. You have room on those mules?" She shot up and skipped to the side of the dock to peer at the pack mules. "Plenty, you've got plenty of room. Just lash 'em down and let the mules complain."

Diego had opened his mouth twice to answer her. He stuttered once, trying to tell her to mind her own business, and then gave up. It would be easier to saddle a bull than to shush Trinidad.

Stackpole grinned. He put up with her every day. Let someone else try for a change.

"Trinidad! Slow down!" Diego said. "We'll see to our own mules."

Trinidad sulked, but her mood changed quickly. "Who wants to have anything to do with your smelly livestock? Hey, y'want to see the new fishing boat we're building?"

She was hopeless, but there wasn't a bit of meanness in her.

Captain Carter made his way up the gangway and sat down with them. He nodded politely and barked something in his clipped, strange English.

Stackpole translated, "He introduces himself: Captain Caleb Carter, master of the brig *Two Brothers*, out of Boston, Massachusetts."

Stackpole introduced the boys. At the name "de la Vega," the captain brightened.

"He asks if you are kin to Don Alejandro de la Vega."

Diego, charged with the honor of the house, rose and bowed to the captain, shaking hands. "Perhaps you will tell him that I am Diego de la Vega, the son of the house. Please extend to him my courtesies and my father's respects."

The captain seemed pleased. Diego suspected that the people of Boston were a snappish lot and glad of even a little kindness.

The five of them, a strange group of sailors and vaqueros, Yankees and *Californios*, sat enjoying the warm afternoon sun and a pot of tea, with and without molasses.

"Can you ask the captain if he will favor us with news of the European war?"

The captain thought, bit off a twist of chewing tobacco, and chewed vigorously for half a minute before answering Stackpole, who translated again.

"He says that King Ferdinand is still imprisoned by

Napoleon, and that they are putting up one of the Frenchie's brothers, Joseph, to be king of Spain."

The captain spat. This news shocked Diego and Bernardo.

"Yes, he says the British are hammering at the Frenchies in Spain."

"Excuse me, Señor *Capitán*." Diego addressed himself to the Yankee, knowing the translation would follow. "My father, Don Alejandro, would be vitally interested in these matters. Could I beg the honor of your company at our hacienda tomorrow evening? Perhaps your countryman"—he bowed to Stackpole—"will come along to translate for you, Señor."

Captain Carter knew something about the hospitality the hidalgos put out. He had eaten mostly salt beef and ship's biscuit for months. This was an invitation not to be missed. He spat again and agreed immediately.

The packages for de la Vega were a parcel of books wrapped in oiled silk and bound in tarred cord, and a small bale of what was probably factory-woven cloth from Mexico City. The boys retrieved them from Trinidad's boat and lashed them to the packsaddles with the pottery.

"Not like that," Trinidad groused. "You use line like a landsman."

"I *am* a landsman," Diego said hotly, snatching the end of a lashing line back from Trinidad, "and I use line like a vaquero."

"You're not getting the line tight around the saddle parts," she complained.

"I don't want them too tight!"

"How tight is tight enough, Diego? As tight as your drawers?"

Diego stopped and looked up, shocked that a young woman would mention his underclothing, but Trinidad merely took his pause as an opportunity to grab the line's end and hitch it tighter.

"There, you big tuna fish. That's the way to lash a line down."

Bernardo chuckled, shaking his head at both of them. Still stung, Diego mounted Lucrecia with a resentful frown. "We're leaving!" he said unnecessarily.

"So go on," Trinidad shouted. She was angry about something else, but what? "And the answer is no! I won't come up to your fancy hacienda and have dinner with the fancy quality folk!" She stumped back onto the dock, broke into a run, and in a few moments was back in her boat, casting off and sailing out.

◆ ◆ ◆

They rode across the peninsula above San Pedro Harbor and down to the beach again. It curved in a long, late-afternoon line toward the wooded bluffs in the northwest. They rode easily and did not speak for a long time.

Bernardo cleared his throat so that Diego looked over. He signed to Diego: Trinidad was upset.

"Yes, I suppose we should have invited her. She is a handful, but she's a good person."

Bernardo nodded.

"But would she be comfortable at our table? Would *Papá* or *Mamá* be comfortable with her?"

They rode on for a time, listening to the deep rumble of the surf, feeling they had each been unkind to Trinidad. On the beach ahead of them, waves broke steeply into the shore. Indian children rode the waves into the shallows, swimming like otters.

"This isn't Barcelona. This is the edge of the world," Diego said. "We've got Spaniards, Indians, Yankees, and even Russians. Every kind and mix. I can't complain about people like Rafael Moncada if I sort people into categories, can I? I should have invited her."

Bernardo rode up beside him and put his hand on Diego's shoulder. Yes, they might act differently next time.

They rode the beach, crossing streams and rivers that met it, shallowed and curled into sandbars. It was April and the sun would set early, but they were close enough to the hacienda to see its kitchen smoke. Estafina would be making a meal for all of them.

They rode on, hoping that the pottery rode easily behind them.

5

THE CIRCLE GAME

ON ALEJANDRO ENJOYED MAKING a grand
entertainment for his guests. Beyond a mere
dinner, he had planned a *Californio* spectacle.
The vaqueros who had accompanied Carter and
Stackpole to the hacienda would play one of their
rowdy, frenzied games for the guests.

Padre Mendoza arrived as wine and cakes were
being passed around the veranda. Estafina's husband,
Montez, tended a barbecue fire. Estafina and her
helpers mopped sauce on great slabs of beef sizzling on
iron grates above the fire. A pot of beans bubbled at the
side.

Diego and Bernardo saddled horses and joined a
dozen vaqueros as they swung their mounts into a
circle, the horses' heads inward.

Stackpole translated Carter's question: "The captain asks if this is the way you begin your polo games."

Padre Mendoza laughed, and Don Alejandro said, "No, friends, this isn't polo. That's a game from the ancient world. This is the Circle Game, one of our *Californio* diversions. It's a bit faster, there are fewer rules, and it's rougher."

Scar walked out to the ring of horses and called to Juan Three-fingers, one of his crew bosses. Juan backed out of the circle doubtfully, and Scar gave him a long bamboo rod, whippy but stiff. He said, "Good luck, caballero."

The other vaqueros chuckled and called out to Juan: "You'll need some goose grease on your back tonight, caballero!" and "Are you ready to weave and duck, brother?"

Juan called back, "We'll see whose back is raw by midnight."

The vaqueros began to whoop and holler as they all faced inward. Each had his good hand open behind his back. Juan walked his big bay stallion around and around the circle, then spurred it into a slow trot. More whooping. Pedro Maduro called, "Come on, Juan, give that soft little feather duster to me!"

But quick as a flash, Juan leaned in and thrust the

40

bamboo into Bernardo's hand. Then the rowdy part of the game began.

Juan Three-fingers kicked his stallion into a gallop. Bernardo pulled his reins, and his horse danced back out of the circle. The pony whirled and charged after Juan. Bernardo almost caught him, and Captain Carter let out a squeal of dread as the bamboo whistled toward Juan's back.

But Juan slid off to one side of his horse. At a full gallop, he held on in some way Carter couldn't imagine. The bamboo struck the saddle with a sharp *thwack!*

All the vaqueros were sitting sideways on their saddles now, watching the fun and the incredible riding skill. These vaqueros loved to show off, but Carter winced at the heavy price they might pay for fancy horsemanship.

Bernardo brought the bamboo up again, but Juan had already righted himself and wheeled his stallion, riding past Bernardo on the other side, heading for the empty space in the circle!

Bernardo's pony spun in the opposite direction and tried to cut him off. The best he could do was land one solid *whack!* on Juan's back before the vaquero skidded to a safe stop in the circle. Juan laughed like a maniac as he rubbed his back. "Only a sweet caress!" he called.

Carter was so excited that he shook Stackpole as he spoke, hurrying the translation: "He says that this is polo if the players used each other as the ball!"

Now it was Bernardo's turn to look worried. The vaqueros whooped and called out to him, facing in again with their hands ready. Diego, mounted on a spotted Indian pony, chuckled at the thought of Bernardo getting a few whacks. But then suddenly Bernardo thrust the bamboo into Diego's hand.

Diego tugged on the reins, and his pony reared back, then tore into a gallop. Diego turned inside Bernardo and stayed between him and the circle. They passed the empty place in the circle over and over as Diego swung the bamboo in whistling circles. Ducking, changing pace, Bernardo avoided all but a few of the blows. "You'll get it now," Diego shouted. He rode up close to whack the daylights out of poor Bernardo, but no! Bernardo leaped completely out of the saddle, holding only the big horn and the flared cantle. He was pulled along on the far side of the galloping pony with bounding steps. The bamboo flailed against the saddle as Diego tried to catch one of Bernardo's hands and dislodge him.

Now the space in the circle was approaching again. Bernardo waited until Diego finished one swing and leaped into the saddle, pulling his pony into a skidding slide. Diego galloped past, and Bernardo walked the pony into the circle to the cheers of the vaqueros and Diego's moans. Now it was *his* turn to fret.

They played until the sun went down and the riders were only blurs. Then Scar gave a deafening whistle and they all rode to the hitching rail, laughing like children. The beaten and beaters laughed together, not a moment of resentment. They were vaqueros and, rough as it was, this was their game.

"Clean up, you filthy cowmen!" Estafina shouted, and they lined up at the stone troughs with their thirsty horses, perching their hats and neckerchiefs on their saddle horns to scrub up.

The vaqueros had begun to load tin plates with barbecue when Doña Regina appeared on the veranda. "Gentlemen!" she called. "Dinner is waiting in the dining room."

Captain Carter would have been delighted with the hearty fare around the barbecue fire. He had been confined for months aboard his small vessel, so anything but a tin plate of dried peas would have looked wonderful. When he saw the dining room, it seemed like a view of heaven. The table glowed with a dozen candles, silver serving dishes and tableware, lace tablecloths and—as always—the striking beauty of Doña Regina. Her thick black hair was swept up and held with tortoiseshell combs. A smile from her high-boned, bronze face seemed to leap out, white and dazzling.

The captain had won the doña's favor by bringing her a printed silk shawl of green and blue, as intense as a peacock's feathers. He was scrupulously polite, but shy and awkward with his beautiful hostess. Stackpole's uniform was clean, though a bit frayed at the sleeves. He carried himself with quiet courtesy that showed he had been a guest at gracious tables before. Padre Mendoza, charming and warm as always, discovered that he liked these Yankee sailors.

Estafina was in the kitchen now. She had worried all day when she learned that she would be cooking for two foreigners. The honor of the Spanish Empire and all of California weighed heavily on her shoulders. She was especially wicked to all of her helpers, and her voice rose hourly.

The fragrant dishes were brought in. Don Alejandro carved a young goat perfectly roasted with raisins and rosemary. It was surrounded by vegetables and the ever-present chiles. There was a great brown loaf of bread, still warm from the stone oven. The padre had brought mission olives and a small cask of the mission's wine, which was served in pitchers with the juice of lemons and oranges.

The captain hadn't eaten this richly in years. He sighed, cooed, growled, and hummed his delight with each mouthful until Doña Regina couldn't help herself. She broke into a happy laugh. "*Capitán* Carter!" she called. "You poor man! Have they starved you all across the great Pacific Ocean?"

His jaw froze. He was shocked. He hadn't noticed what noises he had been making. He was suddenly afraid he had offended his hosts, but Don Alejandro's friendly chuckle encouraged him. He broke into rapid chatter and Stackpole translated.

"The *capitán* apologizes for his loud offense. A man who has eaten weevily biscuit and beef from a salt barrel for a year shouldn't be allowed to dine with civilized company. He sadly admits that your delicious food has shown him to be a brute."

Don Alejandro broke into laughter. "Tell the *capitán* that such a brute may sit at my table any evening!" The don tore into a bite of goat and gave such a growl that everyone at the table laughed again. Then he said, "I worry only that you will give our dear cook, Estafina, an exaggerated view of herself. Estafina!" he called. "Estafina! Come!"

Estafina appeared from the kitchen with a worried expression. The Boston captain rose from his place at the table. He bowed over her hand and kissed it, then grinned and said something that didn't need translation: "Mmmmm!"

Big Estafina blushed, dipped a girlish little curtsy, and disappeared back into the kitchen, giggling.

As the dishes and the tablecloth were being taken away, Doña Regina rose. The men and boys stood for her. "Señores," she said, "I will leave you to your coffee and cigars," and she swept from the room.

A silver pot of coffee appeared. Scar entered, carrying a polished cedar box of cigars, which he offered to the Bostonians and the padre. At a nod from Don Alejandro, he took a cigar himself and sat just behind the don, near the table. The boys could see that he was here for a reason.

Diego and Bernardo got up to go, but the don motioned them to sit down. This was a change—being invited to sit with the men when they were about to talk some kind of business. But they were not offered cigars.

The conversation went remarkably well, partly because Stackpole was a good translator, but also because Don Alejandro guided it deftly.

He asked about the situation in Europe. The well-informed Captain Carter, speaking through Stackpole, described Napoleon's attempts to bring Spain under his thumb. He explained the iron shackles of rules and punishments that kept the French tyrant in power.

Stackpole continued: "The captain says that his countrymen, and especially Bostonians, are no great friend to despots of any kind. Nor are they—with the greatest respect for your views—great admirers of kings."

Don Alejandro nodded, puffing his cigar. "The *capitán* might be astonished to know how much I value independence and the rights of the people. True, I am sworn to be a soldier for the king of Spain. But not for Bonaparte."

When this was translated to Carter, the captain rapped on the tabletop with his knuckles, a kind of applause in agreement.

"These are strange times in our pueblo," Don Alejandro continued, and the boys could sense that he was coming to his purpose, "hard times. Something or someone is taking our cattle. Good craftsmen are disappearing. Who will help us? Not Spain. With Napoleon's war, Madrid is even farther from California than it was. We *Californios* are no longer the children of

Spain. Perhaps we will never be again."

More rapping of knuckles.

"We are practical men, *Capitán*."

The Nantucket man looked thoughtfully at the don through the cigar smoke, guessing at what might be coming.

The don went on. "The letter of the law on this coast is that we are forbidden to trade with foreign vessels. Yet agreements are made. We're almost without a government. The official packets from Acapulco and Panama haven't arrived for months."

Padre Mendoza nodded sadly as Stackpole translated.

"There are things we need, *Capitán*. Trade goods, simple things. Let us arrive at some agreement between us. Not to defy the law, but to nourish the pueblo."

Stackpole translated, listened, and gave the captain's reply: "He is agreeable to all free trade, especially with a man of honor."

Don Alejandro bowed in thanks to the compliment. "What if I were to deliver hides and tallow to the *capitán*'s vessel, a cargo he might sell almost anyplace. He could return with goods we need. If the *capitán* places his trust in us, we will place our trust with him."

The captain smiled warmly and held out his hand to

Don Alejandro, who took it as warmly.

Bernardo and Diego looked at each other: secret agreements at our table!

The don said, "Today in the pueblo, this year's mayor beat the drum and announced the day our *apartado* begins next week. This is our spring rodeo. We will be parting out and counting the mission cattle and the cattle belonging to the ranchos. We will brand our calves, make a fiesta, and then we can slaughter the needed number of steers for the hides and tallow. Most will be de la Vega cattle. The padre and I have arranged that some will be mission cattle, so that his necessities can be met, since he has lost several hundred head of cattle. All this will require three weeks of hard work. Can you return at a given time when the cargo is ready?"

Stackpole translated, listened, and spoke. "The *capitán* asks me to express his gratitude for the don's trust in his discretion and fidelity."

The men shook hands all around while the boys watched. Just being allowed to stay in the room was a mark of the don's respect for them. It was his way of bringing them into the difficult and confusing world of practical matters.

Scar disappeared to arrange for horses and an armed

escort back to the docks. Even around a prosperous pueblo like Los Angeles, there were still cougars, wolves, and marauding grizzly bears. More dangerous than natural predators, the bandit El Chollo had robbed a traveling party of soldiers to the south; who knows where he could be tonight?

At the hacienda door, Captain Carter asked Stackpole to translate one more question: "He asks if you or the padre have seen or heard of his ship's cooper, his barrel maker, Mr. Warr. He came ashore to arrange for water yesterday and has not returned. He is a reliable man and unlikely to desert his ship in a foreign port. If you see or hear of him, please contact the captain or me."

The padre crossed himself and said, "Another craftsman has disappeared!"

Stackpole translated a question from Captain Carter. "He asks if there is some wickedness afoot in the pueblo."

Don Alejandro glanced at Scar and the padre. He puffed his cigar and blew out a thin stream of smoke as he thought. "We have the makings of a mystery, for sure. But at the edge of the world, there are always mysteries, yes?"

The men exchanged handshakes and compliments.

Stackpole and the captain mounted awkwardly. With hooting and shouts, the vaqueros galloped out of the hacienda with the two sailors clinging to their saddles.

Scar, the padre, and Don Alejandro talked quietly on the veranda.

The boys stood with them for a time, but they were tired. They walked around the hacienda toward their sleeping porch.

"Bernardo," Diego said.

Bernardo stopped and looked at him.

"What is happening to all these reliable men who disappear?" Diego mused aloud.

The two boys pondered this mystery as they drifted off to sleep.

─ᖾ 6 ᖿ─

"APARTADO"

BERNARDO WOULDN'T RIDE A mule this day. Before dawn he and Diego rode out of the hacienda on experienced cow ponies. Behind them they trailed their *remuda*, a picked string of extra mounts.

The fortune of the pueblo was on the hoof. Every hidalgo, padre, and neophyte depended on cattle. Hides, tallow, and meat were the only wealth *Angeleños* had. Everything from the distant world was bought with stacks of cured hides, bags of beef-fat tallow, barrels of salted meat. Blacksmith, potter, baker, carpenter—every life in the pueblo was somehow tied to cattle.

In the next week, the boys and men of Los Angeles would live in the saddle. Three or four times a day, each would return to a moving camp and step down from an exhausted horse. Each would shift a big-horned working saddle to a fresh mount, then return to the herd and dust and hard riding.

By mid-morning the de la Vega vaqueros had made their first sweeps of foothills, steep ravines, and wooded bluffs on the northern edge of the rancho. They combed out cattle and calves—along with white-tailed deer and some ill-tempered wild pigs.

The boys stayed near Scar and the crew of Juan Three-fingers as they rode in and out of dense scrub brush, up and down canyon slopes.

To town riders the vaquero outfit might look merely colorful. But townsmen didn't ride through brush like this. The vaquero's short rawhide chaps and leather leggings slid through thorn and branches that would have taken the skin off an unprotected rider. Even so, the caballeros were often hung up in vines. They cut themselves free with the straight-bladed knives tucked in their leggings.

It was noisy work. Whooping and calling, chucking and whistling, they drove the cattle south toward the open country. When they emerged from a canyon with half a dozen or twenty head of cattle, another crew would drive them toward larger herds farther south.

The first crew would move to the next section of rancho to coax de la Vega stock into the open.

The boys had worked up a streambed and were trying to move one stubborn beast.

"How can anything be as stupid as a cow?" Diego demanded.

Bernardo shook his head: No, nothing is as stupid. He whistled and slapped with the coil of his reata—his lasso—against his chaps: Get moving!

"Out of there!" Diego shouted, but the frightened creature was backed into a corner of rock and trees with branches above.

Bernardo made a loop and a good toss with his reata. But it caught on the branches. Nothing to do but get down from their ponies and push the stupid cow out, probably getting a foot stomped for their trouble.

Juan Three-fingers rode up and leaned down to look at the situation. "A stubborn one, I see," he called amiably. He reached behind the cantle of his saddle and uncoiled a black whip. Bernardo and Diego backed their ponies out of the way. Juan tossed the whip out behind him, where it lay like a sleeping blacksnake. Then his wrist twitched forward.

Pop! The tongue of the whip cracked just behind the cow's flank like a pistol shot, and the cow shot from the corner like a cannonball. Juan smiled after it. "Stubborn? I'm more stubborn."

He nudged his pony with his knees and rode away, coiling his whip.

"Saints and cats and little fishes," Diego said to Bernardo. "That's something we've got to learn!"

The cattle were just naturally stubborn. If they were herded in one direction, they wanted to go in the other direction. On foot the situation would have been hopeless. Only the ponies made it possible.

"Cow ponies are just a little smarter than cattle. Only a little," Scar had told them, indicating a tiny amount with his gloved fingers, "but it's enough."

Enough made for some fancy riding. When a cow pony confronted an unwilling cow, the rider's job was mostly to stay in the saddle. He might give an occasional hint from his knees or the reins as to which direction the cow should travel. The rest was up to the horse. Dancing this way and that, the pony anticipated the cow, breaking into a few dainty steps, whirling to meet a new rush back toward the brush. The rider's work was to swivel and sway on top, just a passenger, while the horse danced the cow into frustrated obedience.

But too often the slab-sided, square-faced, bloody-minded, sharp-horned creatures broke away for a long run back to the brush. Then a vaquero took over. Diego leaned into his pony's turn as a big bull made a run. His hard-braided leather reata whistled above him a second or two, then flew ahead of the bull with coils unfolding behind it. The bull ran into the loop, which tightened around its neck. Diego's hands flashed as he dallied—took turns of the reata around his saddle's big horn. The cow pony skidded to a stop and waited with its legs braced. Surprise. The slack popped out of the line, and the bull's momentum jerked him back and up into a backward bull somersault. He landed with a meaty thump and a puff of dust. Diego backed his pony and the bull rose, unsteady at first. It moved in the direction Diego was pulling it, deciding that this was a fine direction in which to travel. As the re-educated bull trotted past, Diego flipped the reata free of his horns and coiled it, ready for another cow and another lesson.

Scar tried to keep one of the old hands working near the boys. Bernardo soon found out why. A younger bull passed them, trying to get back to the brush.

Bernardo took off after him, whirling his reata, coming closer and making a good catch. He dallied, hurrying to get turns of line around the saddle horn, and backed his horse. But this bull was running at a different angle. Instead of jerking backward, the straining line drew him into a circle, back toward Bernardo. Then the bull charged.

"Whoa there!" Diego called, but Juan Three-fingers was already in motion. His reata curled out low, its loop rolling on the ground. The bull ran across the loop. Juan gave a twitch and then took his dallies. He had the bull by the hind legs. When the slack ran out, the bull was caught forward and behind.

Bernardo's horse had been pivoting to run, and the boy had almost thrown the dallies off his horn. But now he and the pony saw the bull go down. Bernardo threw another quick turn on the horn, and the angry bull lay stretched out on the ground.

"Now what?" Diego called.

"We'll just hold him a bit. Let him forget what he was angry at. Then he'll be as sweet as a lamb. Won't you, *toro*?" Juan reached down and twitched his loop loose. As the bull rose, Juan freed Bernardo's loop, then let his pony dance back. "Get on with you, now! Hoo!" he shouted at the bull. Dazed, it ambled toward the other cattle moving south.

Juan Three-fingers walked his horse over to Bernardo. "Exciting?" Bernardo was wide eyed. "Pull your glove up tight there, and be more careful how you take those dallies when you rope," he said. He held up his three-fingered hand. "You don't want to get any fingers caught in that reata, boy." He grinned and rode away.

Diego's fingers tingled and he pulled his gloves up tight too. Both boys looked at their saddle horns with new respect.

They herded bulls, cows, and this year's new calves. Diego and Bernardo worked steadily south with Juan Three-fingers's crew. The rancho's territory seemed even larger than they thought it could be. By noon they were exhausted, resting in the shade, almost too tired to eat the bread and meat laid out on ground cloths.

At the end of the first day, they had covered only a small part of the rancho. The cattle were tired as well. They seemed content to stand and chew as if they'd been there all along, not dragged and hallooed and forced out of every thorny nook in the foothills.

The light was fading when Diego and Bernardo rode into the field camp. The cook fire was bright where big iron pots hung from iron rods. They unsaddled their mounts—the fourth of the day—and rubbed them down with dry weeds. They staked them out with the rest of their *remuda* in good grass, checked their hooves, looked for cuts or bruises, and fed them some barley to go with the sweet grass. Only then could they drag their saddles near the fire.

The iron pots sat on the ground now, and the vaqueros sat around them. There were no plates. Each vaquero produced his own horn or wooden spoon and ate broth from the stew pot. Larger pieces of beef were caught up with corn tortillas, sometimes dipped in a pot of bittersweet *mole* or fiery salsa.

When they had eaten, Scar called in the men who had been walking their mounts slowly around the herd. He sent Diego and Bernardo to saddle up again. They would be the early-evening nighthawks, night minders of the placid cattle.

There was most of a full moon. The herd, hundreds of cattle now, made a constant low noise of breathing, sighing, jostling, and the occasional clack of horns. Their smell was big and musky but warm. Diego saw bats in their quivering flight against the moon, and once an owl. Coyotes called from the foothills where they'd ridden all day.

"I wonder where the coyotes were when we rode through there?" Diego asked. He often voiced his thoughts aloud, not expecting any response from Bernardo.

59

"That was something the way Juan Three-fingers shooed that bull away from the cliff with his whip."

Bernardo remembered the horseman's skill.

"He uses that thing like a long hand, doesn't he?"

They both sat their horses, quiet. Without a word, they both started to walk around the herd in opposite directions. They didn't need talk to decide most things; that's the way they were together.

Diego walked his horse and sang a little, trying to remember a song about the sly fox going out to catch the farmer's goose. The fox probably went out on a moonlit night just like this, he decided. He met Bernardo on the far side of the herd, away from the camp, and they passed each other without even nodding, continuing their rounds. But just seeing each other was comforting. It was good to have a brother. Wouldn't life be lonely without a brother?

There were so many stars!

7

EL CHOLLO

IN THE MORNING DIEGO and Bernardo were comb-
ing cattle out of little valleys above the Camino
Real, the king's official road. Bernardo looked up at
the sky. The vultures were with them every day, always
riding the wind above them, but this circling funnel of
vultures signaled that something was dead.

"Looks like we've got a dead cow." Diego sighed.
Nasty business. The most valuable part of the animal
was the hide, so a vaquero's job in this case was to skin
the dead cow.

They rode on, hoping the beast hadn't been dead
long.

They trotted along the road, sending up dust behind
them, and rounded a bend where it followed the shoulder of a rise. They pulled up their horses quickly. It

wasn't a dead cow but a dead man.

"¡Madre de Dios!" Diego said, not wanting it to be true.

Bernardo whistled and whirled his reata, riding toward the vultures. They scattered and flapped clumsily into the air. But they didn't go away. They circled, waiting.

Bernardo backed his pony away from the body and pointed to a grove of trees. They tied their mounts there and ran to the body. Diego was about to rush up to it, but Bernardo stopped him, holding up a finger: Wait a moment.

He circled the body at a distance, looking closely at the ground. He picked up some broken twigs, a clump of weed, and a few leather strips. He circled inward slowly. Finally he knelt by the body on the ground and motioned for Diego.

"It's Señor Porcana, the potter," Diego whispered. The vultures hadn't done much damage, yet. "He must have died last night." Diego swallowed hard.

Bernardo tried to lift Porcana's head, but the body was stiff. He bent close to the ground to look at the blood-clotted hair. He showed Diego the wound, then made a sharp chop with the side of his hand: He was murdered.

Diego looked closely at the wound and nodded. "And look at this." Porcana's strong hands were still clenched in anger. The knuckles were raw; skin and hair clung to the nails. "He was a tough little man, and he fought back."

Bernardo pointed to the wrists, chafed and bruised, then held up the leather strips. He showed Diego the frayed place where the strips had been rubbed through.

"So he was tied up, broke free," Diego said, "then fought and . . ."

Bernardo gave a final chop, then held out his hand to the body: And here he lies.

Pointing to the ground around the body, Bernardo held up three fingers and made motions of riding away fast. Then he pointed south, toward the pueblo.

It took time for Diego to recover enough to speak. "Why would anyone kill Señor Porcana? He was irritable, but not a bad man. And he was the best potter we have. We needed him."

They looked at each other.

"And Paco Pedernales!" Diego said. "Another craftsman missing, like Padre Mendoza's tanners. Like Captain Carter's cooper. All skilled men! But why?"

Diego looked again at the bruises on Porcana's wrists and the marks of his fight. The answer jerked him back like a reata around a bull's horns.

"Look!" he said to Bernardo. "Señor Porcana is speaking to us, just as clearly as you speak to me without words. He is telling us that the missing men were taken, kidnapped. They had to be: he was tied up. He struggled to get free. When he got free, he fought the men who captured him. That's what happened to all of them."

Bernardo squatted on his haunches, clasping his hands together, deep in thought.

"But why? Why capture Porcana, a potter? A carpenter like Pedernales? Tanners, barrel makers . . . Why?"

Bernardo thought some more, then looked up at the vultures.

"Yes," Diego said, glancing up, "I'll ride to the camp and get a packhorse for Señor Porcana. You stay here and keep our flying friends away from him."

Scar and Don Alejandro rode back with Diego. They trailed a mule with a packsaddle and a length of tent canvas. Porcana had a family in the pueblo and would be buried near the mission.

When they rounded the bend in the road, they saw Bernardo sitting beside his saddle on the ground, playing his flute. His horse was tethered in good grass a hundred paces away.

The older men looked at Porcana's head wound. It was hard to turn the stiff, awkward body over, but when they did they found a knife wound in his chest. They looked at each other seriously.

"From what we saw on the ground," Diego said, "we think he was here with three other men. Señor Porcana was bound, broke free, fought with them, and was killed. Then the men rode away quickly toward the pueblo."

Don Alejandro looked closely at the body and pointed to the neck. A pale shadow in his tanned skin showed where something had hung, probably a religious medal. Then he said, "This man was an artist. More than just a potter. His work was beautiful."

"That's just the point, *Papá*. All the men who have disappeared are skilled workers, craftsmen, artists. Doesn't the way Señor Porcana died tell us that they've been captured and taken away for something? The real mystery is why. Who needs all these skilled workers?"

Don Alejandro looked at his son thoughtfully and was about to speak, but Scar brought the canvas. Respectfully, quietly, they shrouded Porcana's body in it and bound it with cord.

They sat on their heels beside the body without talking. Then Don Alejandro said, "One craftsman might leave for better pay, a new woman, or just to see what's on the other side of the mountain. But this many men? No. The pattern is too strong. And if this is another pattern"—he gestured toward the body— "they were captured violently. Were they all killed? Doubtful: they could have killed Porcana easier when they first tied him up. But why are they capturing men?"

Scar finished lashing the cord around Porcana's canvas shroud.

"Here's one possible explanation," Don Alejandro said. "To start a new place—a colony or settlement— you must have skills. That's what the padres did. They brought skills to every settlement along the Camino Real. Every mission was a new beginning. They taught the important skills to all their neophytes."

Diego thought a moment, then said, "If someone is trying to build a colony, why don't they recruit craftsmen in Mexico City or even Spain? Why take our craftsmen?"

The don pulled at his earlobe, then said, "Here's what I think. Somewhere in or near our pueblo, there are ruthless men who want their own colony or settlement. Let's call it a kingdom or dictatorship, because it's not a lawful settlement, not a civilized place. That's why they can't do it openly. Their only method of getting skilled men is slavery. Most craftsmen are free men. They might buy a few talented slaves from the plantations in the United States or from Jamaica, but that would cost a fortune and take too long. They want to build a new place now, and rule it soon. They're willing to do anything to make it happen."

Don Alejandro looked up at the vultures. "Some men are just like the vultures. Maybe there are other explanations, but I can't think of one now."

Scar nodded his agreement, and Bernardo nodded his.

"We wouldn't know this much without him." The don patted Porcana's stiff shoulder through the canvas. "We owe much to our brave potter. Or we will, when we solve the mystery."

Diego was about to speak again, but Don Alejandro held up his hand. He shifted from his heels to kneel in the dirt. The others did the same. They crossed themselves, and Don Alejandro prayed aloud for the soul of Señor Porcana.

When they reached the mission, Padre Mendoza washed the body and wrapped it in white cotton.

When Señora Porcana arrived, it was already laid in the chapel on planks, and padres were chanting prayers around it.

Friends were digging a grave in the cemetery. Porcana was respected, an old member of the pueblo, one of the first neophytes. His wife stood weeping outside the door of the chapel when a man walked up to her and passed her something with a murmur. She looked at him, and Diego heard her say, "*Gracias, amigo.*"

The man began to move away into the shadows. Diego stepped quickly to Scar. "Who is that man? There, by the prickly pear in the churchyard. Who is he?"

"Humph!" Scar said scornfully. "That is a man of no honor. El Chollo, the bandit. He lives in the hills. We see him in the pueblo rarely. Some of the people have a fondness for him because he seems adventurous, a rebel. People are easily misled."

Diego walked past Señora Porcana, bowing, and then toward the churchyard, motioning for Bernardo. They broke into a fast walk, and Diego whispered, "I just saw the bandit El Chollo give something to Señora Porcana. I saw it in Señora Porcana's hand. I think it was the medal Porcana wore, the one that was missing from the body!"

They half ran through the churchyard, as quietly as they could in spurs, and went through a small door in the rear, hoping to see El Chollo's horse riding away. Perhaps they could follow and spy on him.

They froze, hearing the double click of a flintlock pistol being cocked just behind them.

"You boys wanted to see El Chollo?"

Diego said quietly and respectfully, "*Sí*, Señor."

"You boys know what cholla is? You don't have it much around here. It's a cactus that likes company. If you put your fingers near it, it doesn't want you to go away. Just a touch and you're stuck. Sticky, painful stuff, cholla. You maybe don't want to mess with it."

"Señor," Diego said, not turning around, "we're not here to bother you."

"You're not bothering me. I'm amused."

"It's just that I saw you give a medal to Señora Porcana. Perhaps the medal Señor Porcana was wearing when he died."

"And you're wondering if I killed Porcana?" he asked.

There were times when Diego's eagerness overcame his good sense. Perhaps, he thought in the split second before he spoke, that's what courage is about and why it gets so many people killed. He gulped and said,

"Excuse me, Señor Chollo, but yes. No one is here with us. We are just boys. You could tell us without involving yourself in any way."

"You don't know much about the world, boys. Another bandit, he might be insulted by the question and blow your brains out. Another bandit, maybe. But there are bandits and bandits. You know why no one has ever caught El Chollo?"

"No, Señor." This was one of the times Diego wished Bernardo could speak, just to take some of the load from him.

"Because El Chollo doesn't rob poor people. They have troubles enough. I rob only the Spanish and the soldiers. I give a little back, even, and some to the church. Enough to buy me some warning now and then."

"So you didn't—"

"Porcana was my friend. We grew up together. I ate his wife's tortillas many nights. I gave that medal to him, and his wife deserved it back. No, I didn't kill my friend. If I find the men who did, they would be better off in a bonfire. I saw them ride off."

Diego glanced at Bernardo. "You were the reason they rode off so quickly!"

"*Sí*, I saw them only at a distance. They were not,

somehow, like our vaqueros. Their style was different, their boots and their hats, small things. So I will be looking for them. And you boys"—he tapped each one on the back of the head with the muzzle of his pistol— "have no reason to come looking for El Chollo, right?"

"El Chollo?" Diego asked. "I never heard of such a fellow. Never heard of him, certainly never saw him. I think he is one of those hill legends, is he not?"

A slow chuckle from behind them, a long silence, and when they turned, no one was there.

After the burial they all rode back toward the camp and the *apartado*. Bernardo was playing his flute mournfully, but Diego knew he would be listening.

"*Papá*, what did Padre Mendoza say about the skilled men and the kidnappings?"

They rode on for a time. Don Alejandro said, "He agrees with us that someone is capturing our craftsmen and taking them into some kind of slavery. Probably to make a colony or a kingdom, as we said. It's vicious, wicked, ambitious, and dangerous. Mexico City won't help us. Madrid can't. We must find a way to unravel this mystery ourselves, *hijos*. Ride carefully from now on. And keep your eyes sharp."

~ 8 ~

THE BEAR

OST VAQUEROS WERE YOUNG men in their twenties. But there were older men, too. A few of them had learned their trade from the old padres, starting as Gabrieleños who had hardly seen a horse. It was a hard trade to learn, but there was a swagger to it like no other. Vaqueros were proud men.

The old hands woke stiff and wrapped their aching knees and elbows in flannel rags to warm them before the sun came. They hobbled to the cook fire for porridge and hot chocolate.

Diego awoke stiff and sore. He rode every day, but he didn't herd cattle on cow ponies: this was another kind of riding that used a new set of muscles. And every one of those muscles was aching. His eyes were crusty and his tongue felt like a saddle blanket.

Bernardo brought him a mug of chocolate and pointed toward the horses. Most of the vaqueros had saddled their first mounts of the day.

"I'll be ready in a heartbeat," Diego said.

Later they stopped their first mounts at a little stream to wash their faces. As they knelt in the sand, Bernardo pointed to a patch of soil nearby. There was a big print in it, still moist and clear.

"St. Bernard's bees!" Diego whispered, then looked quickly around for danger. "That's one big grizzly bear! I don't want to meet him, and for sure not in a gully like this. Let's get out of this streambed."

They splashed another handful of water on their faces and mounted up. Then they heard the roar and the squeal.

It was a deep, throaty rumble, as loud as a landslide. The squeal was from a horse in pain. Diego's horse sidestepped nervously, but he touched the flanks with his spurs and got up the slope.

A stone's throw away they saw a massive grizzly bear, as big as a haystack. His brown, loose fur quivered and shook as he roared again, one massive paw on the neck of a downed horse that was kicking feebly, screaming in pain. Some of the camp's tethered horses had pulled

73

out their stakes and were galloping away, trailing their tethers between their legs. Some of the stakes held. The horses tied to them reared and screeched, their eyes almost all white in terror.

Diego was frozen, so frightened he couldn't move. He could see Bernardo in the corner of his eye, just as terrified by the awful spectacle.

Over the earsplitting roar, they heard whoops and drumming hooves. Scar, Juan, and most of the crew galloped almost right up to the grizzly. It was difficult for Diego to understand, but they seemed delighted.

The grizzly's rubbery nose was turned up, and his lips pulled back to bare his teeth as he stood his ground. He wasn't giving up his prey. The bleeding horse whimpered; the tethered horses continued to scream.

The vaqueros circled, their reatas whistling above their heads. Scar's was the first to dart out, tightening around the bear's thick, shoulderless neck.

The bear swiped at the reata, sending a jerk along it that jolted Scar and his pony, but they held firm as Juan's loop folded around the bear's head over Scar's. Both men dallied and backed down their ponies. The loops tightened.

The grizzly's roar rose. He wanted to swat these new

creatures with the snaking vines, but their vines choked him. Angrier than ever, he rose on his hind feet, bellowing defiance.

Mesmerized, the boys leaned back in unison. A grizzly on all fours was big. A standing grizzly was huge, taller than a man on a horse. They had only heard of elephants, but they couldn't be any bigger than this!

The bear dropped down on all fours to make a charge, but as soon as his hind leg rose for another step, a third loop from Pedro Cinque caught it. Another loop caught his neck. Another snagged his forepaws as he swiped the air. The circle of ponies backed down unsteadily, straining at the live load. The grizzly toppled to the grass, bawling and flailing.

Diego's mind was working at an incredible rate. He saw everything sharply, in the same way that ideas and solutions sometimes came to him. The grizzly's claws were as big as boot knives. He could see the wet, quivering nose, the big pouchy cheeks, the tiny eyes set deep.

The vaqueros were excited. This was their own grand sport. Spaniards could talk about bullfights with their fancy *matadores*, but let them come to California and see a real contest! Here a few vaqueros and their cow ponies made sport of tying down the biggest, strongest predator anywhere.

Juan Three-fingers sang out a long, excited yelp. "Keeeee-yi-yi-yi! Look at this big fellow! He is bigger than a mountain! He could eat a ship! And angry! This big, hairy fellow wants to eat all of us for lunch! Be careful there, Bernardo! You are just big enough for this bear to pick his teeth with!"

The crisis wasn't over. If any one of these reatas broke, there would be big trouble.

Pedro, one of the young vaqueros, was jumping with excitement. "This big *oso* will make a good fiesta spectacle. We can put him in a ring with some bad bulls and watch them fight it out! It's not far to the pueblo, Jefe," he called to Scar. "Let us drag Señor Oso to the mission stock ring for the fiesta."

Diego and Bernardo had seen bull-and-bear fights. They didn't like them. For some it was a fine spectacle, letting brutes fight each other. They were both dangerous enough. Rampaging bulls and surprised bears had killed a few *Angeleños*, true enough. But it was a messy, sad show. There was no real point. The bear always won, killing bull after bull. Sometimes it tired and was gored by a fresh bull in the end. It was a cruel thing, taunting something wild.

Scar sat on his straining horse. He shook his head no.

It was too far to the pueblo, all day to drag and tease a bear to the mission's stock ring. That was too much danger for his men and their horses. And for what? Still, this big raiding bear couldn't be allowed to eat the rancho's horses whenever he wanted a meal.

"Diego!" he called. The boy rode around the circle of vaqueros and reatas to Scar. "My horse," he said. Diego leaned down and took the reins of Scar's horse.

Scar swung down from his saddle, taking the short musket, the *carabino*, from behind his saddle in the same movement. He checked the flintlock, looking at the priming powder before he walked into the circle, approaching the bear. He brought the musket up, cocking it, steadied its aim, and fired. There was a double ball of white smoke, one from the musket's flintlock, one from its muzzle. The big bear quivered, grunted once, and sank to the ground like a tent with its pegs knocked out. No one moved for a long moment.

"Stay away from him," Scar said. The dead didn't rise, but the dead weren't always dead. He walked back to his horse, the only person not looking at the bear. He took his powder horn and bullet pouch from the pocket of his saddle's *mochila* and quickly reloaded the musket. Then he waited a few more minutes.

No one slacked his reata yet.

It was quiet for a time. Juan Three-fingers had stopped the grunting and labored breathing of the injured horse with his boot knife. The scene had become almost peaceful.

Scar approached the bear from behind and prodded it with the muzzle of the *carabino*. Nothing, no movement. He nodded. Now the reatas slacked and the vaqueros stepped down to loosen their loops and coil them. Juan opened the jaw of the bear and shook his head with a little shiver, looking at the yellowish-white teeth, terribly big.

"Juan, round up those horses." Scar pointed in the direction they had bolted. "Esteban, Julio, Carlos, Arturo—keep working these next valleys." They mounted and galloped off in their excitement.

Bernardo looked at Scar and waited.

Scar nodded, as if to himself, then glanced back at the bear. "Big fellow. Big enough for a rug," he said. "Pedro!"

The young vaquero stepped down from his horse.

"You and the boys skin Señor Oso out. Drag his carcass over to that ravine and put some brush on it."

Scar was a mestizo. His mother had been a Gabrieleño. The bear was a sacred animal, part of the human family. It was well known that the most power-

78

ful sorcerers, perhaps even White Owl herself, had at least one bear parent. They were respectful of bears, even in death.

Pedro nodded.

"Then back to work." The vaquero nodded again.

"Bernardo, Diego, you wrap up the bearskin tight and cut out a good pony." He gestured to the horses Juan was rounding up. "Pack the skin on the pony and ride up to White Owl's village. Give her the horse with my compliments. Ask if she will have some of her women prepare the hide and the head for a rug that will go in the hacienda, yes? The horse should be enough payment for curing the hide and bringing it down later this week." Scar looked up at the sun's place in the sky. "You can be up in the village before dark and join us down near the river by late morning."

Pedro tied his horse to a sapling and took off his jacket, hat, shirt, and sash. The boys did the same. It would be a long, bloody afternoon.

9

THE VILLAGE

BY LATE AFTERNOON DIEGO and Bernardo were up out of the grasslands and into the forest. Mile by mile they rose into the cooler air of the mountains. The trail was narrow but well worn. It followed a streambed that tumbled out of the peaks in a long, singing series of little waterfalls.

Late in the afternoon, they began to see charms hanging from the trees—a doll made of tied grass, a bird skin spread on a forked stick, quartz rocks in a little net. These bits of local magic announced the presence of a shaman, a sorcerer, so that evil spirits would stay away from the village. Perhaps it worked, because White Owl's village was almost always a peaceful place.

Now they saw the red ocher paintings on boulders

framing the trail and knew they were entering the village.

Entering a Gabrieleño village was not like riding into a pueblo. It didn't start with corrals and buildings and shops. Except for the charms and the markings, it didn't seem to start at all. The village was a kind of living circle for spirits. It was not just where the homes were, but a larger place for things that could be seen and things that could only be imagined.

Smoke curled through the trees ahead. They smelled the sweet, pitchy pine smoke from the sweat lodge fire. Then they heard whoops and loud, happy voices. As they came into the clearing, half a dozen voices called to them, "Diego! Bernardo!"

A shouting knot of thrashing runners, their sticks clattering against one another, rushed past them. They had ridden into the middle of a lacrosse game. The leather ball shot out of the crowd, and an out runner seized it with his netted stick. Everyone ran after him.

A boy at the edge of the pack spotted Diego and Bernardo. He yelled to his teammates, "Now we'll beat them. We take Bernardo."

"Not when we have Diego," another boy replied.

Diego held up his hand as if holding them back. He replied in Shoshone, "If we don't pay our respects to my grandmother first, she'll turn us into cockroaches."

Snow Wren, the wife of their friend Otter Tooth, was watching the game as she sewed a deerskin bag. Bernardo spotted Light-in-the-Night seated beside Snow Wren. She barely raised her eyes from her sewing, but in the brief exchange of a glance, Bernardo's heart pounded.

"I like to hear boys show respect," Snow Wren said. "And good sense. We'll see you later at the fires, then. Your grandmother is fixing a meal for you."

Diego shook his head and looked back at Bernardo. It was a little annoying that they couldn't make a surprise visit to the village. One way or another, the village always knew they were coming.

They walked their horses into the neighborhood of houses. It was a parklike area of cleared ground under trees. A few of the homes were simple brush lean-tos, but most were high domes thatched with rushes. A few larger lodges were near the center of the village, decorated with colored rushes woven into the thatch.

The very heart of the village was the holy circle, the *yovaar*. White Owl stooped out of a tight little beehive-shaped house beside it. "There you are, finally," she said gruffly. "I haven't seen you for weeks. You don't pay much attention to your grandmother." But they could tell she was happy to see them.

The boys walked to her and bowed their heads so she could place her leathery palms on them as a blessing. "Well, it's good you're here safe," she said. "Give me your horses. I'll put them near some grass. I've laid out clean things inside so you can take a bath before we eat. You're filthy."

"Grandmother," Diego said, "we have an errand from our *mayordomo*, Scar."

"A good, decent man," she said, as if most of the people living on the grasslands weren't.

"He sends you this horse and asks you a favor. We were forced to kill this angry bear." He put his hand on the pelt slung over the packhorse's back. "We don't think it was anyone in disguise or a sorcerer. Just a bear grown tired of his own place in the forest."

"Sometimes a bear is just a bear," White Owl conceded. The Gabrieleños thought that she and her fellow sorcerers could turn into bears if they wished. Diego didn't think it was likely but knew that his grandmother wouldn't argue about it.

"Scar believes it will make a good rug for the hacienda. He knows that the tribe has some skillful tanners. Could they prepare it and bring it down to the rancho later this week?"

She ran her hands through the thick, dark bear pelt.

83

"My daughter will approve. There is some power in a good bear rug," she said. "Scar is a good man. But impatient," she said. "He wants everything yesterday. We will prepare it in the time it takes to prepare it well. This is all I will promise him. And the horse is a good trade." The boys nodded. "Now get those filthy things off and sweat yourselves clean. I have made something for you to eat. Not much. A few scraps."

As she walked off with the horses and the pelt, Diego said, "The worse she talks about her cooking, the more she's worked at it. I wonder what she's made us?" Bernardo smiled, thinking how hungry he was.

A few minutes later, wrapped in rabbit-fur blankets, they walked to the sweat lodge.

As always, a happiness came over them in the village. It was like no other place. Every villager knew them. But it was more than just knowing their names: they knew their mothers and their grandfathers, their family histories, and the long lines of ancestors many generations back. Though the village was made up of many clans, it was one ritual family. What Diego and Bernardo felt here was acceptance, a loving embrace.

A sure thing about Gabrieleños: they were either taking a bath or thinking about taking a bath. When they weren't eating or thinking about eating. They were a humorous, comfortable people, and part of their religion was staying clean. Next to Gabrieleños, the pueblo vaqueros were pigs in the mud.

Outside the sweat lodge, they hung their robes on pegs driven into a pine trunk. Naked, they poked through the hearth embers next to the lodge. There were still some hot rocks. They picked them up with wooden tongs and carried them into the lodge. They dropped the rocks onto the inner hearth and sprinkled a bit of water onto them, then sealed the door again.

They sat in the hot darkness. Their eyes began to accept the dim light from cracks in the mud-plastered rushes. Diego didn't speak, because the sweat lodge was a place to think and turn inward. They sat in the sweltering air, their labored breathing making a companionable whisper.

The sweating cleansed their skins like nothing else. But their time in the heat and darkness was an important meditation, too. Diego found himself remembering his tribal initiation rites when he wandered the forest in a kind of trance, searching for his special spirit guide. He had found his totem animal—the sharp-eyed fox—*el zorro*—with its clear sight and wily ways. The fox was surely a part of his soul. Bernardo found the horse—strong, reliable, loyal, and brave.

After a time, the heat became too intense. Just as they burst out of the sweat lodge, ready to leap into the sweetly cold water, Light-in-the-Night emerged, quietly disappearing like a shadowy forest creature. Bernardo found it hard to breathe, but Diego pushed him in the water. Soon they were diving and splashing and dunking each other. Diego loved being with Bernardo in his grandmother's village. His milk brother seemed freer, more playful here, as if some invisible cloak of sadness were lifted from his body.

They waded out of the pool, dried off, and walked toward White Owl's hut wrapped in their furs, glad for the warmth against the evening chill.

If White Owl cooked something wonderful, it would be impolite to make it only for her boys. So they ate with Trout Spot, the *tomyaar*, both of his wives, and his family in the *tomyaar's* big lodge beside the holy circle.

They ate tender little quail stuffed with piñon nuts, sage, and acorn meal. There was a hot soapstone bowl of cattail roots, wild onions, rosemary, and berries. A bowl of herb tea was set out, and little pots of tangy sauces. They ate from White Owl's best dishes: big, gleaming abalone shells, their holes closed with carved wood plugs and pitch. They ate with lip smacking and grunts of pleasure. These were polite noises of appreciation.

"White Owl, you are a true sorceress. You have made these quail sing in my belly," the *tomyaar* said. "You are an argumentative old woman and a pain in my hip, but you have your moments."

This was the kind of nipping tease that Gabrieleños enjoyed.

"I don't know how you can tell good food from bad food," the old woman said without looking at him. "You drink so much corn beer that you could be eating horse dung."

Everyone laughed, including the *tomyaar*. He and White Owl were old adversaries, but they respected and needed each other.

When everyone had eaten and washed themselves, the rest of the village began to arrive. This was why the *tomyaar* had a large house. There were games and songs, many old jokes, stories, and gossip.

White Owl was gathering up her abalone shells. Diego motioned to her and to the *tomyaar*. They sat against the wall with Bernardo, a little outside the celebration.

Diego said, "There is some serious business in the pueblo. High on the hill here, you see a long way.

Sometimes you know things about the pueblo we don't hear or see."

"I'm a shaman; I see everything," White Owl said.

"Not everything," Trout Spot growled.

"I'm getting old," she said. "I once saw everything."

"I'm sure you did," he said, but he didn't sound convinced.

"Someone is stealing cattle, and someone is stealing people," Diego said. "The rancho is missing hundreds of cattle. So is the mission. And many skilled workers have disappeared. Men with families. Men of trust who wouldn't just leave."

"What does your father make of it?" White Owl said. She had great respect for Don Alejandro, perhaps because he had tamed her wild warrior daughter—something she had never managed to do.

"He's puzzled. His best guess is that someone or some group is trying to set up a colony. They need craftsmen to make the colony self-sufficient. The don worries there may be some kind of slavery going on."

"So where does my son-in-law think these colony makers are going?" White Owl asked.

Diego shrugged. "He doesn't know. He knows only that if they are kidnapping these men, it can't be a legal colony."

"And where are all these cattle going?" Trout Spot asked. "We'd be fatter if they were coming here."

"No one knows. Cattle rustling is one thing, but slavery is an evil matter."

The old woman and the *tomyaar* nodded strongly.

Trout Spot opened his palms as if he were laying out a plan. "Many animals or people must be moved by sea," he said. "The roads are bad, and it would be too easy to spot them or track them on roads. I'll ask some of our coast brothers. They are on the water at all hours. If something moves, they'll see it. And I'll ask our brothers in the mountains behind us, in case I am wrong about moving by sea."

"Too often wrong," White Owl said, poking him in the ribs.

"They killed a man," Diego said, "our potter, Señor Porcana." This news left a silence after it.

"Wicked!" Trout Spot said. "Slavery and murder. Tell Don Alejandro that the tribes are with him in this thing. We will be watching."

White Owl slipped out quietly a little later. When Diego and Bernardo walked back to her hut, she had their reed mattresses laid out beneath her raised bed shelf. Their vaquero clothes were neatly laid out for the morning, and their rabbit-skin blankets were folded down, ready for them.

The fire in her hearth was never large, and now it was little more than a few embers. The house was dim, and White Owl was taking the horn pins out of her white hair.

"Grandmother," Diego said, sitting down on her high bed beside her, "I love being with you." She gave a little shrug as if it was fine for him to say this, but she really didn't care that much. Bernardo sat down on her other side. They put their arms around her and she put her hands over theirs, so that the three of them sat and rocked quietly for a few minutes.

When she had crawled into her sleeping platform and pulled the deerskin curtains around it, Bernardo and Diego lay down on their mattresses with just their heads pushing out from under the platform. The domed house had a smoke hole open to the stars. White Owl's shaman tools hung on pegs with many other things: a cloak of feathers, charms and rattles, bound bunches of herbs, skulls of animals, baskets, deerskin bags. It smelled smoky and herbal and familiar.

"You like Light-in-the-Night. I see the way you look at her," Diego said.

Bernardo kicked his milk brother and rolled away on his side.

"Hey!" Diego complained.

"Hush," White Owl barked above them, "or I'll wet the bed."

The boys giggled, pulled the rabbit blankets up, and closed their eyes.

~ 10 ~

THE TALLY

THE HERD WAS ENORMOUS now. They could see the dust cloud above it long before they saw the cattle. Closer, they heard it, loud with a constant bawling.

A herd this size, thousands of cattle, was difficult to move. Every rider the rancho had was in the saddle. From the shoulder of a rise, Diego could see Don Alejandro working beside the vaqueros, keeping the big, dark mass together. Crews were turning back cattle at the sides of the herd. And coming up behind was the drag—the vaqueros who pushed and worried at the tails of the bawling cattle, keeping them moving in the choking dust. Everyone in the drag had their bandannas wrapped around their noses and mouths.

Bernardo pulled his bandanna over his nose and

glanced toward the back of the herd.

Reading his movements, Diego said, "Yes, you're probably right. We've been up in the mountains taking it easy. Scar will put us on the drag all day."

And he did. "All rested?" he called over the noise. "Get back to relieve a couple of Juan Three-fingers's boys in the drag."

They found Juan using his whip to encourage the slowest cattle, popping it behind them. But now and then, they saw a particularly stubborn cow leap forward, stung.

"Scar sent us to relieve you and a couple of your crew." It was surprising how loudly Diego had to shout to be heard over the sound of the moaning, jostling cattle.

Juan nodded and started to ride off but spun his pony back. "Here," he said to Diego. "Give it a try." He handed Diego the coiled length of the black whip. Then he disappeared into the wall of dust.

"Hoo hoo!" Diego called, and hefted it. He tossed the whip out behind him and gave it an experimental flick, almost knocking his own hat off. "This will take some time to learn," he shouted, then leaned into his pony's turn as it moved across to block a wandering cow.

Both boys were standing beside fresh ponies, spitting, trying to get the feel and the taste of the dust out of their mouths. Diego was gargling a big mouthful of water when Don Alejandro rode up with Scar.

"I'm not sure, caballero, but you look a little bit like my son. Hard to tell with the dust and the dung. But maybe." He grinned from the saddle. "And you, vaquero, I know a boy named Bernardo who resembles you. But his skin is darker, not so dusty white."

Bernardo slapped his jacket, raising a cloud of dust.

Diego spit out the mouthful of water. "We're working in the drag, *Papá*. Hundreds of cattle try to sneak past us, but we hide in the dust and leap out, howling like wolves. They run back to their friends. Bernardo and I are learning to be shape-shifting sorcerers in that dust. We turn into wolves and bears. Anything that will impress the cattle. But you know what frightens them most?"

"What's that, my dusty shaman?"

"We turn into *mayordomos* with big mustaches. It scares even big bulls silly."

Scar raised one critical eyebrow and puffed through his mustache.

"How is the herd shaping up for numbers, *Papá*? Did we have a good spring for calves?"

"Not as good as we'd hoped. With this much grass and the mild winter, we should have hundreds more cattle than we're driving. It's puzzling. We'll sort it out."

"Will the branding begin tomorrow?"

Don Alejandro swung down from his mount and tightened his saddle girth, speaking as much to Scar as to the boys. "Don Honorio is the *administrador* this year, and a few of the garrison sergeants are his *jueces de campo*. I hope they're at least sober. I have no faith in *mataperros* as field judges." He used the rude term for the garrison soldiers: "dog killers."

Scar snorted. It was his short and complete opinion of the soldiers.

"But with this many cattle, they can't go far wrong. God has been good to us. God loves California."

"Yes, and so do we," Diego said, slapping a cloud of California soil from his chaps and jacket. "We love it so much we carry it around with us."

Don Alejandro shook his head. "My son the clown. I would love to sit and laugh at your antics, caballeros, but there is this rancho I must run, so adios, and have a good lunch of dirt, yes?" He and Scar rode off.

Diego and Bernardo spat a few more times, tightened their bandannas, and rode back into the dust behind the herd.

◆ ◆ ◆

The de la Vega herd for this year's *apartado* was assembled. More than eight thousand head of cattle made a satisfying display. Not every cow, bull, and calf had been gathered. There were some wily cattle still grazing in the hills or hidden in cottonwood thickets. Not all of them were de la Vega cattle, either. The herds mixed and wandered. A few hundred of these cattle would carry the cross-and-G of the mission's brand. Some would be branded with Don Moncada's elaborate poppy brand.

When the *jueces de campo* sorted them out, they would find cattle belonging to ranchos far and wide. But the big plain *V* of the de la Vega rancho would be on most of them.

And there would be this year's increase, too. Every unmarked calf the de la Vega vaqueros rounded up would become de la Vega cattle as soon as the branding iron marked them. This was the law of the range.

The herd was backed against the Santa Monica hills. It was time to brand this year's calves. Instead of the great dust cloud of moving cattle over the plain, there were individual plumes of smoke rising from dozens of small, hot fires where the iron brands had been heating in the coals since first light.

But the field judge had to signal for the start. Scar was impatient but reluctant to question the *juez de campo's* authority. "Sergeant Figueroa is still damp from soaking in a bowl of wine last night. We've got to persuade him that he's alive enough to get things rolling. Diego, take him a big mug of coffee."

Diego and Bernardo could see Sergeant Figueroa sitting against a tree, asleep. The vaqueros had long since finished their porridge and coffee, and the camp cook was clattering around in his wagon, starting things for the midday meal. Diego picked up a mug and was about to fill it with thick, sweet, vaquero coffee when Bernardo headed over to the cook's camp box and picked up a pot. Diego stepped quietly toward Bernardo. The pot contained tiny chili peppers, dried almost black, hotter than the Devil's pillow. Diego shook several into the mug and crushed them with a wooden spoon, then poured in the coffee.

The sergeant was snoring. Diego put the coffee beside him and backed away. "Sergeant Figueroa!" he called. The fat soldier jerked awake and looked around, disappointed he was not back in the garrison kitchen, where he usually slept in the morning.

"Shall I fetch you a cup of coffee?" Diego asked. "The one you have there may be cold by now."

Figueroa felt the mug. "No, young de la Vega. No, it's just right for drinking now. I was waiting for it to cool a bit, you see."

Diego nodded and walked back toward the horses with Bernardo. When they had gone a dozen paces, they heard a bullish bellow behind them. "Whoo! Whoo!" The sergeant leaped up, threw the coffee mug into the fire, then began to dance around the tree. "Whoo! Whoo!" He was very lively for a fat man. He took off his hat, waving it to fan his mouth. "Whoo! I'm dying! Bring water!" He was waving both arms as he danced around the tree.

Diego called to Scar, "The *juez de campo* is signaling us to begin, Jefe." But by then every vaquero within three hundred paces had seen the signal and mounted up. Their tough ponies were moving toward the herd, reatas whistling above them.

Back and forth. A hundred times, it seemed, each boy rode into the herd. His leather reata curled out and, when he was lucky, snared a calf. He dallied turns on the saddle horn and backed out, dragging the new member of the de la Vega herd toward the fire. The calf balked and bawled, jerked at the reata, and planted its short legs, but it was no match for the pony. By the fire, one vaquero seized the calf by its tail and back leg, another by the head and front leg, and toppled it. One would sit on its head while the other grabbed a rag-wrapped iron from the coals and pressed it into the calf's flank. For a moment it sizzled and smoked, and then the branded cow was released. They shooed it away from the herd toward the open plain. A few minutes later, it was grazing as though the morning had been uneventful.

The boys roped and they branded. There was no comparison. As hard as the riding and roping was, the calf wrangling was harder. Some of these brutes had grown to the size of a dinner table, and not one of them was cooperative. Toppling a frisky cow was work, and the smell of burning hair was awful.

They were sweating by the fire as Juan Three-fingers dragged an especially large calf toward them. Bernardo looked toward the mission with a wistful expression.

"You're right, Bernardo," Diego said. "Today is the first day that being a padre seems like a better idea than being a vaquero."

—❧ II ❧—

WILDFIRE

A S DIEGO AND BERNARDO rode in to change
ponies, Scar whistled for them. He was looking at a small book with Sergeant Figueroa.
They stood some distance from the camp because the
sergeant was still mad at the cook about the coffee that
he was sure almost killed him.

The boys stepped down from their ponies. Diego
said, "Jefe?"

Scar showed them the book. "Here's the tally of
cattle and calves so far. The good sergeant has agreed
on the numbers. I want both of you to take this tally
book to Don Honorio at his camp on the Moncada
range, somewhere to the northeast of the pueblo. Bring
the tally book back by way of the tar springs. Julio
Castillo's crew is herding there and may need a couple

of extra vaqueros to finish up. We'll see you by last light. The cook camp will be over by the river marsh then. Questions?"

Diego repeated their chores, then Scar said, "Good. *Vayan con Dios, hijos.*"

Sergeant Figueroa spoke up. "And if you see Sergeant Velásquez, tell him I'm out of wine."

The boys touched their hats in respect and replied, "*Sí, Sargento,*" though they had seen Scar's lowered brow and slight shake of the head: No more wine for Sergeant Figueroa until the *apartado* was finished.

They saddled fresh horses, filled their canteens, and rode east to make a sweep of the foothills, looking for this year's *administrador*, Don Honorio.

The pueblo could boast about its twenty thousand head of cattle. Within the sound of the mission's biggest bells were several hundred vaqueros hard at work. Yet this great landscape still seemed empty. Except for the little wisps of smoke from the branding fires, there was little sign that anyone lived here. It was so big and empty that they might have been among those first Spaniards to visit this place. Diego had the strange feeling that he and Bernardo were seeing it just as Padre Junípero Serra had seen it when he came up from Mexico City, long ago.

Diego looked across the peaceful plain. "Don Alejandro tells me that the streets of Barcelona are all pushed together for miles. The shops along them stand wall to wall like the boxes in a stable. Miles and miles."

Bernardo signed quickly: Not for me.

"We'll see it, Bernardo. Before too long we'll go to Barcelona and learn to be fine gentlemen as well as vaqueros. We'll see all those streets and shops and fine ladies. And many wonders, I expect. But Pueblo de los Angeles could never be like that: streets and shops and hard paving everywhere. No, this is the real California."

They came up onto a little crest. Bernardo whistled softly. Smoke was rising behind a stand of trees.

"I don't like it either," Diego said. "That's too much smoke for a branding fire. Something's not right."

Both boys flicked their long reins and spurred their ponies into a gallop toward a thickening bank of gray smoke.

They rode out of the trees into a little meadow. It was alive with flame. A wildfire! This was a cattleman's nightmare—leaping and spreading, burning up the cattle's feed, crippling the pueblo's prime business. A disaster for every *Angeleño*.

The fire was spreading out through the yellow-dry grass, and a thicket of brush was blazing. "It's still small!" Diego shouted over the pop and crackle of the fire. "We might head it off!"

Bernardo looked around for help. He pointed to where, across the fire, dim through the smoke, half a dozen vaqueros were galloping away!

"Where are they going? Don't they see we need help?" Diego shouted.

Bernardo spurred his pony and rode back toward the trees. Diego did the same. No time for dithering!

"The brush! Let's cut a break in the brush! If we do that, maybe we can do something about the grass fire!"

Leaping down from their ponies, they drew their big blades. A young gentleman might carry a sword by his saddle, but a brush knife was more useful to a vaquero—as long as an arm, thick and wide. They tied off their ponies, away from the fire but nervous in the smoke, and ran toward the brush.

Bernardo sprinted around the thicket to the other side. He would cut inward so they'd meet in the center. Let it have half the brush. They'd try to starve this fire.

Diego began a few dozen paces from the fire, cutting carefully. He threw branches, dead wood, and heavy grass away from the fire, trying to make a lane the fire couldn't leap across. He stopped for a moment and looked back to the trees where the ponies were whinnying in fright. The top leaves of the trees were still. Good! The afternoon wind from the mountains hadn't begun yet. As long as the wind didn't blow, fanning the fire toward them, they had a chance. He bent saplings hard over and cut them off close to the ground. Tossing the young trees and their leaves away from the fire, he moved on to the next piece of fire food.

The smoke eddied and rolled. Diego coughed, and his eyes stung. Pulling the bandanna up over his nose and mouth helped only a little. The heat was scorching.

Once he jumped back as a rattlesnake coiled just beneath him, striking and missing. "Look out, *culebra*! You're no help! Get out of here. Save yourself!" Diego seized a chopped limb and whacked at the snake. It slithered quickly away, and he started cutting again.

Now he could hear chopping ahead of him. Yes, and Bernardo coughing. He whistled. Bernardo whistled back, and they kept hacking toward each other.

One moment he could barely see Bernardo. The next moment he had to step back to stay out of his blade's swing. They had made a fairly straight lane across the thicket of brush, but not wide enough.

"I'll widen the break!" Diego shouted. "You try to stop that grass fire!" Diego began to cut at the edge of the break, widening it by another arm's length. With luck, with no wind, he might have time to widen the whole length of the break.

Bernardo ran toward the whinnying ponies. They hated the smoke and the fire. He couldn't blame them.

He mounted his pony and patted it gently, trying to pour confidence into the frightened beast. Riding around the meadow outside the spreading fire, he found what he needed: a fallen tree. It was a handsbreadth thick in the trunk, dead for several seasons, no leaves. Bernardo hitched his reata to the trunk and dallied the end to his saddle horn. When he pulled back, the tree moved without much difficulty. He turned the pony and moved ahead, pulling the tree behind them. The leather rope burned across his thigh, squeezing it painfully, but he didn't have time to think about it.

The tough cow pony shied and danced away from the flames. Bernardo fought the pony's fear and his own as he rode along the burning edge. The dead tree's branches dragged across the fire, mashing the grass down, kicking up sparks but stubbing most of the flames out. He rode one way and another along the black edge until he and the pony were exhausted. But they had stopped the fire.

Bernardo tied the pony in the trees again and ran

back with his brush blade. He stalked the edge of the burn, stomping embers and kicking apart clumps of smoldering grass, digging into smoking pockets with the blade and scattering the bits of fuel. Breathing so much smoke had made him sick. He coughed painfully and threw up.

The fire wasn't as loud as it had been. He could hear Diego cutting brush and coughing. The firebreak had worked. The fire was burning itself out.

The afternoon wind finally swept in. The cool air was welcome. But it also blew up new sparks and fanned old embers into flame. They worked for hours at the stubborn fire. A dozen times it threatened to revive itself and devour the great plain.

"Any more water?" Diego asked, shaking his own empty canteen. They were both lying against the trunks of trees near their horses, gasping and trying not to cough, more tired than anyone had ever been. Or it seemed that way.

Bernardo gave him his canteen, which had a few drinks left. It tasted wonderful. Anything that didn't taste like smoke was wonderful.

They helped each other up and walked toward the center of the black, burned ground. "Here's where it started," Diego said, then spat several times, trying to get the grit and dryness out of his mouth. "Those vaqueros that rode off started the whole thing. At least we'll know what rancho they ride for," he said, stooping to pick up the warm branding irons.

They looked at all the irons. "No we won't," Diego said. "I've never seen irons like this before. There's no brand here I recognize. Do you?" They weren't real brands but curves and circles and squiggles.

Bernardo shook his head: None that I know.

Diego looked around them. "I think the fire's out now. And Don Honorio still needs the tally book. Unless an angel in a chariot will deliver it for us, we've got miles to ride."

They gathered up the irons and walked back toward the trees and their horses. They had their arms around each other, partly out of brotherly affection but mostly to stay upright.

Don Honorio was sitting under an oak tree sharing a pitcher of wine and fruit juice with Don Moncada when the boys rode up.

"*Hola, hijos,*" the *administrador* called to them as they approached. "Where have you been? Have you been digging in the mines? You're as black as Barbados fishermen."

"*Sí*, your honor. We have been digging in our gold mines. It is messy work, as you see. But the profit is too great to ignore. We will put up with a bit of blackness for a bit of gold, yes?"

When the boys came closer to them, Don Moncada wrinkled his nose at the sour smoke smell. "Truly, Diego, what has happened to you?" He was more polite than his son, and much more charming.

"We stumbled onto a wildfire, Señor, and paused to put it out," Diego said.

The older men were concerned by his news, but Diego went on. "It was not a big fire as such things go. It was just our size. Large enough to frighten us, small enough to put out, and nasty enough to turn our stomachs."

Diego handed Don Honorio the book.

"The fire was begun by some vaqueros," Diego continued. "They were branding calves with brands I have never seen. We brought them with us. Perhaps you will recognize them."

"But first we must see to our brave young fire-eaters," Don Moncada said quickly. "While our *administrador* copies the numbers of your tally, I will have your horses watered and seen to. You will sit down with some cider or juice to clear your throats. It is only right. I insist." Such a hospitable demand could not be politely refused. Diego and Bernardo bowed, and Don Moncada pointed them to a tent near the cook camp. "I will have my vaqueros see to your horses and join you in a moment."

It was cool in the tent, and there were elegant folding chairs. Moncada arrived with an Indian servant bearing a tinkling tray with pitchers, glasses, and pastries. Bernardo's eyes were wide in appreciation. Diego smiled, gulped down the sweet juice, and worried about smudging the cloth of the chairs with his sooty clothes. In a few minutes, Don Honorio joined them, carrying his large tally book under his arm. He handed Scar's smaller book to Diego.

"I have recorded the numbers, young de la Vega. The *apartado* for this year is nearly complete. We can look forward to the fiesta now."

Diego rose and said, "With God's blessing, we can be hopeful for a good increase of cattle. Yes, and we will have a grand fiesta. But, with respect, gentlemen, we must return to what duties remain. Our *mayordomo* is, you know, a man of iron will. We must be where we are told to be." He bowed again, and they all walked out of the tent.

Bernardo's horse was waiting, but a hard-eyed

vaquero the boys had never seen offered Diego an unfamiliar horse and saddle. "Excuse me, Don Moncada, but this is not my horse," Diego said.

"We had a minor excitement," Moncada said. "Your horse, a fine mount, must have been upset by the fire. When my men tried to rub it down and give it some water, it bolted. Galloped clean away. I had a few vaqueros ride after it. They'll bring it back to your hacienda tomorrow, along with your saddle. Until then, please accept the use of a Moncada mount and one of our saddles."

Diego paused a moment, then his natural courtesy returned. "Many thanks, Don Moncada. You do me a kindness with this beautiful stallion. I will use it with respect for its bloodline and for your generosity. Again, *muchas gracias* and adios. *Vayan con Dios.*"

"Yes," Don Honorio said, "go with God."

The boys rode west toward the river in silence. After a while Diego said, "It's a good horse. But I'd sooner ride my own horse."

Bernardo looked over his shoulder to the distant Moncada tent. He made the sign for trickery.

"I bet we'll never get those irons back. That must be why Moncada took my horse. The irons are a clue to something."

Bernardo pursed his lips.

"Did that vaquero who brought this horse look a little strange to you? Did you see his boots and chaps? They're not local gear, are they? A bit foreign?"

Bernardo looked at him, looked back toward the Moncada ranch, and whistled low and soft.

The sun was only two handsbreadths from the horizon. They flipped the reins against their horses' necks and headed for the river marsh.

12

PRACTICE

IT HAD TAKEN HOT water and harsh soap to scrub
away the last traces of the smoke from their hair.
Their shirts and pants were riddled with burn holes
from cinders. Estafina whiffed their boots with a disgusted face. "The smoke will preserve these boots for-
ever. Unfortunately."

"Ah, but Estafina," Diego said, "think of the good
work we'll be doing. Wherever we go, sinful folks will
smell our boots and think of the fires in hell. They will
mend their wicked ways and take up charitable works."

"God shouldn't hear you! Reminding people of
hell! You are a strange boy, Diego. Bernardo, you should
light a candle in the church for your odd milk
brother!"

Their throats were still smoke raw and they still had

burns from flying embers, but they would rather fight the fire again than face the awful task ahead of them: dancing.

They stood like convicts in a row before the fireplace: Diego; Bernardo; Regina; Estafina; her husband, Montez; Francisca from the kitchen; and the laundress, Gracia. With Don Alejandro, they made four couples to practice the pattern dances. The furniture of the big room had been pushed back against the walls. Two of Padre Mendoza's neophytes sat with guitar and harp to make the music.

"A true gentleman is graceful on a horse, on the fencing mat, and on the dance floor," Don Alejandro insisted.

The boys groaned. Regina groaned. But the don would not be discouraged: the house of de la Vega would present itself with elegance at the *administrador's* ball. Every hidalgo, soldier, and Spanish lady would attend this high point of the *apartado* fiesta at Don Honorio's hacienda.

"Dancing is a conversation in movement," the don lectured them, "and it must be played out in rhythm. Light but restrained. Casual but deliberate. Balance, flow, grace! Now form two lines: ladies on this side, gentlemen over here. Thank you all for filling in."

113

He walked them through the geometry of the dance without music first. The head couple joined hands, bowed, and stepped down between the lines. Then the next couple. When all the couples had gone down the line, the ladies joined hands and formed a circle. It went on and on. Diego wanted to die. He was certain that any one of his cow ponies could do a better job at this dancing business.

But when the harp and guitar played the lilting Spanish tunes, it was a kind of game. They made mistakes, they tripped now and then, but the dance played itself out and they were all laughing, breathless with the effort. They sat on the window seat and panted. As a game it was not all bad.

The don put his hand on Diego's shoulder, his forehead damp with the effort of dancing. "Dancing. It may feel silly at times. I promise you this, though: as much serious business has been settled on a dance floor as on a battlefield. Maybe more.

"This is social business, a show of confidence. A gentleman who proves himself on the dance floor and in the dining room can be more powerful than a merely skillful swordsman."

Diego and Bernardo looked at him, not quite believing. He must have seen their doubt. "A steady blade and fighting skill will go a long way. A gentleman who can manipulate a conversation as well as his sword point can be truly powerful. And truly dangerous." Don Alejandro laughed. "The deadliest swordsman I ever knew was also the best dancer. Swordplay and dancing require the same things: rhythm, balance, timing, confidence, and a bit of audacity. It all goes together."

Regina rose and drew her skirts up around her, then began to chant. She was singing in the Shoshone tongue, and began the flat-footed, shuffling, beat-beat-beat dance of the Gabrieleños. Estafina and Gracia leaped up to join her. The neophytes played the rhythm on harp and guitar. Montez began to clap out the rhythm, then the boys and even Don Alejandro clapped as the women turned and turned in a Gabrieleño corn dance, faster and faster. They collapsed on the window seat in a breeze of laughter and panting. The men applauded.

When their breath returned, Don Alejandro got up again. "Now we do a dance from Madrid, the slow paseo dance in a circle. Women on the inside, men on the outside."

Bernardo's head drooped. Diego cried, "No! You mean there's more than one dance?"

◆ ◆ ◆

Bernardo found Diego sitting beside the fountain pool, his fists balled, his eyes damp with tears. He sat down and put his arm around Diego's shoulders.

It was hard for Diego to speak for a few moments. Finally he said, "I'm not going to the fiesta. And I'm surely not going to the stupid ball at the Honorio hacienda. No. Never."

Bernardo looked at him, waiting: Why not?

"My new clothes. Embroidered pants, buttoned seams. Fancy little jacket and sash. Ridiculous. Stupid."

Bernardo shook his head: That's not the reason.

"No. It's not. My finery is hanging in the sewing room beside your new clothes. Except you don't have a hidalgo's suit. Yours is a cotton smock with braid and a blue sash. I asked *Papá* why you didn't have a suit as well. He told me that you wouldn't be coming to the ball. You would be outside with the servants. The servants! As if you weren't good enough for the highborn hidalgos. I told him I wouldn't go anyplace you couldn't go. Period. He called me foolish and stubborn."

Bernardo nodded: He's got a point there.

"It's not right. It's not fair. Did you know you weren't allowed to go to the ball?"

Bernardo looked down at the paving stones. They

116

said nothing for a time. Then Bernardo nodded again: Yes, I knew.

"Then I don't go either."

Bernardo shook his head hard: No, you're wrong.

"Why should I go? Why, when I'd be making myself part of something so unjust?"

There was only the sound of the fountain for a time. Bernardo turned. He took Diego's shoulders in his hands, as if to tell him that something was important.

He laid his left hand on his own chest and then sent it curving out to the left in the sign of a path: I take a path.

He put his right hand on Diego's chest and his hand curved out to the right: You take another path.

Both of his hands curved out. But this time they met each other. They joined, and their fingers locked together: You go your way, I go mine, but our paths meet. We are together, we are always together. He looked hard into Diego's eyes and nodded: This is the way it is; this is what we have.

Diego looked away and tears came into his eyes again.

Both of them sat beside the splashing pool without speaking for a long time. They watched the shadows of the vines stirred by the Pacific breeze and signed with each other. They had made a pact.

A little later Bernardo got up and made the sign for hunger.

"Me too," Diego said, and they went to the kitchen.

13

BLACKBIRDERS

"I HAVE BUSINESS IN THE pueblo," Don Alejandro told the boys the next morning. "I must arrange for more workers if we are to supply our Boston captain with tons of hides, tallow, dried beef, and salt beef."

Diego nodded and said, "*Sí, Papá*," but there was a sullen silence around his words. Regina looked up from the tea she was pouring, hearing the tone in his voice.

"I would be happy for your company," the don said.

"*Sí, Papá*, I will ride with you," Diego said. A cool curtain had fallen between father and son since Diego had learned Bernardo wasn't welcome at the ball.

"Both my boys," the don said, "I would like both my boys with me. I value their company. This would please me, the three of us together." He left the room, leaving

Regina, Diego, and Bernardo standing at Estafina's worktable.

"I need a few things from Señora Vestido's shop in the pueblo," Regina said. "Perhaps you will pick them up for me. I'll make a list."

Diego nodded, not speaking, hardly looking up from his plate.

Regina reached in front of him and rapped her knuckles on the table. "Listen with more than your ears, boy. It can be more difficult for a warrior to say some things"—she nodded her chin toward the door that had closed behind Don Alejandro—"than for a tailor or a carpenter. Sometimes you must listen very hard to hear an apology." She looked at both boys. "You may learn this someday. Or you may be too hard-headed. I'll make my list." She too left the kitchen.

The pueblo was almost crowded. Lanterns were being hung for the fiesta, and the shops were busy.

The boys tethered their horses and loosened their saddle girths. Don Alejandro turned from his big mount. "Scar has been talking to his crews, arranging"—he laid a finger on his lips to indicate a secret—"what must be arranged for our Boston friends. He will join us here. The four of us can sit down to a meal.

Both of you go ahead to the inn and see to it. Perhaps they will make us some chicken tamales or some beef steaks. Whatever you choose. I have business with Señor Pérez."

The boys walked toward the plaza. Bernardo touched his heart and looked back toward the don: I love that man.

"And he loves you. I know he does. But he is set in his old ways. Old Spanish ways. Old hidalgo ways." Diego shook his head, angrier at social fences than at the don.

They walked along the line of carts and stalls at the edge of the plaza. Farmers and craftsmen sold fruit, dried beans, chiles, rice, dyed leather lacing, horn combs. They could have walked all afternoon, talking to their friends and hearing the news of the pueblo. But a shriek came from the inn. The boys broke into a run.

A young woman ran out of the shadows of the vine-trellised tables, sobbing. Five deeply tanned men ran after her, grabbing at her skirts, laughing and crowing, "Come back, *chica*! Come sit on my lap! I like little girls!" They were loud, showing off, drunk enough to be dangerous. "Come back, *chica*, and we'll whisper sweet things to you! Come back

121

and bring your *mamacita*."

They were not vaqueros, not soldiers. With their pigtails and tattoos, they had to be sailors, strangers to Pueblo de los Angeles.

The girl ran right past the boys, not even seeing them in her fear. Diego had the spark of an idea. He pushed Bernardo right into their path. Bernardo was surprised but suspected some Diego trick. He stumbled to a stop just in front of the sailors, holding up his hands sternly: Stop right there!

The sailors were startled. They stopped for a few heartbeats, then the biggest sailor said, "So you're bossing us around? What this Indian needs, shipmates, is some face decoration. I can give him some fancy stuff," and he reached for the knife on his hip.

Now Bernardo looked worried.

Diego grabbed Bernardo by the shirt and began to beat him, blow after blow. *Whap! Whap!* The sailors fell back, first in amazement, then they began to enjoy the sight of one Indian brat being beaten by another.

It was a game the boys played, pretending to fight fiercely but hardly touching each other. When Diego threw a punch with one hand, he struck his side with the other hand, making a meaty *whap*! The trick was to react to a punch that never landed. Bernardo jerked his head back as if he had been struck. They scuffled. Now Bernardo broke free and threw a punch at Diego. He slapped his side just as his fist passed an inch from Diego's jaw. Diego jerked back, shouting, "Oof!" They couldn't play this for long. The sailors would be expecting some blood with these mighty blows, but at least the girl was safely away. Diego wrestled Bernardo to the ground, shouting, "Grab at my sister, will you?"

The sailors were confused a moment longer. The Indian hadn't been grabbing at the girl. *They* had.

But Diego dragged Bernardo to his feet and held him by the shirt collar. "We'll see what the *comandante* says to a dog like you! Molesting young women and these fine sailors! Come with me, you hound!" He began to drag Bernardo back toward their horses.

It almost worked.

The boys had moved only a few steps when the big sailor kicked a chair over in their path. "Well now, shipmates," he said to the others, "we come for a drink and get a show. These boys figured we're just as dumb as farmers. But we aren't stupid corn diggers. You country boys want some advice? Play your games on dirt farmers and Indians. Not blue-water men and blackbirders. We seen all kinds of games. We shipped a thousand blackamoors between Africa and Jamaica, and we seen it all. Every trick that can be played. Not so easy to fool us. Maybe you give us a show, but you're going to pay for it." The sailor moved toward them, slow and menacing.

"Aha!" Diego cried, trying another diversion. "The seafaring man is not amused by our little charade. And we worked so hard to please you! What can I do to gain your favor? Can I produce a coin from your pigtail?"

He reached behind the sailor and seemed to pull a coin from his hair. It was a bit of hand magic that White Owl had taught him to entertain the village children.

"And look"—he held the coin up—"there isn't even a spot of tar on it!"

The sailors frowned in puzzlement.

"But I thought that tar ran in the veins of every sailor man! Every hair a rope yarn, every finger a marlinspike—isn't that what they say? So every vein a tar bucket?"

One of the sailors actually smiled, but he may have been more drunk than the others.

"Why don't he say nothing?" One of the sailors pointed suspiciously at Bernardo.

"There is a sad tale, friends," Diego said. "Our

mother told him, when he was very young, not to speak unless he had something interesting to say. He's been waiting all this time—years it's been!—to find something really interesting to talk about. This is one of the reasons we arrived to amuse you. I said, 'If these far-faring seamen aren't worth a comment or two, you're hopeless!' But, as you see, my brother remains unmoved and silent. Personally, I find you highly colorful and even awe inspiring. Your tattoos alone are worth a book. And there must be a story left behind from each of your missing teeth."

Diego plucked another coin from behind the ear of the sailor who had asked about Bernardo. He polished the coin on his shirt. "They're small coins, but bright enough to call for a pot of ale, don't you think?"

"That's enough out of your piehole!" The big sailor batted the coins out of his hand and they rang against the wall and bounced twice on the cobbles. One came to rest at the boots of Don Alejandro.

"Gentlemen!" His clear voice turned the sailors' attention. The don stood tall in his fine suit and red sash. "Gentlemen, you have us at a disadvantage, yes? We do not even know your names. You are strangers to us, and already you are displeased with our pueblo. Let me introduce you to some of our citizens. I am Don

Alejandro de la Vega." He bowed.

"This fine gentleman is my *mayordomo*, Esteban Cicatriz." The sailors turned to see Scar leaning against a fig tree, with his short saddle-musket cradled in his arms.

"Behind you, there, is one of my high-spirited vaqueros, Juan Three-fingers." Juan was coiling his long, black whip with close attention.

"The vaqueros on your other side, there, are part of his crew." Four vaqueros in their spurs and chaps stood gazing at the sailors with their reatas over their shoulders.

"My large friend, Señor Ortega, is our blacksmith. You have not met him, but you must know his daughter, because you invited her to sit on your lap." Ortega walked in from the street with his sledgehammer, his eyes as hot and angry as coals.

"I myself have no daughters. But these two rascals"—the don beckoned to Diego and Bernardo, who walked carefully away from the group of sailors—"they pass as my boys, foolish and troublesome as they may be."

The sailors were looking about them nervously now.

"We all make mistakes. I believe we have begun on the wrong footing. My suggestion is that we start fresh another day. It is a long walk to the port of San Pedro, and this day is half gone. Perhaps you need to be on your way, yes?"

The sailors backed away from Don Alejandro. Without another word, they made a wide circle around Juan's vaquero crew and started down the dusty street at a rapid walk.

Don Alejandro put his arms around his boys. "I have known good generals who don't have your flair for delaying tactics," he said, then laughed. "Señora Ruíz!" he called to the inn's mistress. "Can you bring us pitchers of wine and juice and some bread for all these caballeros and for Señor Ortega? We are dry after chasing squirrels away!"

~ 14 ~

THE FIESTA

ALL DAY LONG THE pueblo had throbbed with music. Guitars, harps, flutes, and drums played vaquero songs, love songs, bandit songs. Little choirs of neighborhood children walked along the streets, singing church hymns in close harmony to earn sweets and coins. Crews of vaqueros, dressed in their finest, showiest clothes, competed with one another in singing. The crowds on front porches and sitting beneath the plaza's trees voted for one crew or another with applause.

Diego and Bernardo were dressed in the new clothes that had caused so much anger. But now they had a pact: these were not clothes, but costumes for a play. They acted in a comedy as master and servant. Anyone who mistook them for an hidalgo and his ignorant servant was a part of the comedy. Anyone they could fool was someone to laugh at later: "Did you see that Spanish soldier bow to me and brush past you without a word?"

Diego played at walking haughtily in front. Bernardo walked behind holding Diego's fine hat like a chalice from the mission church. Bernardo would stumble against a passing soldier so Diego could pretend to be furious. He smacked his clumsy servant in their game of fake blows. Diego punished him so severely that one visiting soldier said, "That's the way to discipline these people!" When the boys walked around the corner, they collapsed in fits of giggling.

They thought these were games they could only play on visitors to the pueblo. But a few local hidalgos believed their game. Worse, they thought it was natural.

The boys sat under the canopy of a blooming pear tree. Diego wondered, "Do those people really think that we could grow up as brothers and just decide to be master and servant?"

Bernardo shook his head.

"Some of them do, though. This is California, not Spain! This hidalgo and peasant thing is unfair."

Bernardo looked in the direction of the soldier they had fooled.

"Well, we seem to do a good job of deceiving soldiers and the duller hidalgos. Do you think we could have the last laugh on people like that?"

Bernardo thought a few moments. He nodded and put his hand on Diego's shoulder: You bet we could!

And that became part of their pact too.

"Now we'll hear some good singing," Diego said.

Their friend José García stepped out on the porch and adjusted his sash. It had to be a very long sash to get around his big belly. He took a sip of water and began to sing. He had the voice of an angel. He sang an old love song from southern Spain. Everyone had heard it, but García made it new. The lovers in the song, separated by cruel fate, were so sad that tears rolled down many cheeks, and women sighed.

For all his belly, García was popular with the pueblo señoritas for his sweet voice, his manners, and his shy smile.

When he finished, the street broke into applause.

"More! More!" Diego cried, and the crowd took up the cry: "More, García!"

"Sing about the fox and the gray goose!" Diego called, and García beamed at him.

"That I will!" he called to him, and began the song.

The crowd hushed instantly. García started the wily fox on his way to the farmer's barnyard and almost got him to the pen where the ducks and geese were kept.

A big ripe melon dropped from the balcony above. It exploded over García's head with a *whop!*

There was a cruel laugh from above. Diego and Bernardo saw Rafael Moncada disappear through the door to the balcony.

The crowd in the street scattered when the melon splashed. A few laughed, and one old woman seemed angry with García for getting her wet and sticky.

Diego and Bernardo helped him to his feet. He was a bit dazed. "Big melon," Diego said.

"What?" García said, still confused. He looked down at his wet clothes. He tried to brush the sticky seeds from his best frilled shirt.

They helped García to a fountain. Bernardo disappeared and returned with a borrowed towel. "Wrong song?" García asked.

"No, it was a good song," Diego said. "You were just an opportunity for Rafael Moncada to show off. He dropped the melon. He's long gone by now."

Bernardo made the sign for sweet or ripe.

"We're lucky it was a ripe melon," Diego said. "A green melon that size might have snapped your neck."

Bernardo nodded at the balcony and made a few signs to Diego.

"Bernardo says something larger than a melon should fall on Moncada's head."

García laughed shakily.

Diego helped him up and said, "We'll walk over to your house with you," Diego said, "and we won't walk under any balconies."

After sundown bonfires blazed all around the pueblo. Each bonfire lit its own celebration. Vaqueros danced high-kicking steps to the driving beat of guitars and drums. At other bonfires they danced with señoritas under the suspicious eyes of their *dueñas*, their chaperones. These were stern-faced aunts and grandmothers who would be furious at any displays of budding romance. Many of them would be furious over and over before the fiesta was finished.

Diego and Bernardo wandered from bonfire to bonfire, greeting their friends, celebrating this year's *apartado* with vaqueros and Gabrieleños.

Late in the evening, they rode to the Honorio hacienda for the hidalgos' ball, where Diego was expected to uphold the family's honor on the dreaded dance floor.

"Well, I'll do my best. That's all I can do," Diego said nervously as they unsaddled their horses outside the hacienda. He brightened up as he whispered to Bernardo, "Ready for the special dance?" Bernardo thumped a big package by his saddle and nodded with a mischievous grin.

The dancing scared Diego. He could fall over his own feet in front of his father's friends. He might disgrace the de la Vegas. ("Their son is such a fool!") His pants would surely split when he bowed. A thousand bad things could happen! The ball loomed like Judgment Day as he walked into the brightly lit courtyard of the hacienda, especially the fandango dance with its elaborate steps. Still, as he passed a large mirror he thought if he covered his large ears, he made a remarkably handsome *Californio*, with tanned skin, white teeth, dark hair, strong cheekbones, fiery eyes. Diego had discovered that he enjoyed wearing fine clothes.

Three things made the evening actually enjoyable.

The best thing happened much later.

The sweetest thing happened immediately: he saw his mother beneath the chandelier, lit by a hundred candles. It's good for a boy to see how beautiful his mother can be. She wore a gown of pale ivory silk that made her skin glow like a burnished bronze bell. Her thick black hair was done up with combs of turtle shell. A mantilla of delicate white lace lay around her broad, strong shoulders. Diego felt proud to be her son.

The most painful thing happened next. He fell in love. The girl was talking to Regina and Don Alejandro, and for a moment he stopped breathing. How could he breathe, looking at this girl?

Regina saw her son and motioned to him with her fan. He would have been glad if Scar had called on him to ride the drag right now. He couldn't possibly walk directly up to a creature like this and live more than a few seconds. He considered running. He could saddle his horse and make it to White Owl's village by morning. He could live there from now on. This was a fine idea. Instead, he walked to his mother.

She kissed his cheek, but he was unaware of this detail.

Don Alejandro bowed to his own son, and then to the enchanting young woman. He said, "Don Diego de la Vega, I have the pleasure and honor to introduce you to Señorita Esmeralda Luisa Avila, come to us from Mexico City. Señorita Avila is the niece of Don Honorio. Alas, her parents have been taken from us by sickness, and she will now be one of our *Angeleños*, living at the Honorio hacienda. She is an accomplished . . ."

The don went on, saying many things, but his voice faded into the buzzing sound in Diego's ears. The sound was caused, apparently, by the exact curve of Señorita Avila's mouth, and perhaps by the painfully perfect shape of her chin.

"Diego!"

"Yes, *Mamá?*" he said, but he was looking at Esmeralda Avila.

"I asked if we might have the pleasure of watching you two dance."

"I would sooner be eaten by ants," Diego meant to say, but what came out was, "With delight, if the señorita will endure my stone-footed attempts."

Don Alejandro beamed. Regina bowed. Esmeralda fluttered her black lace fan. Diego remembered to raise his left hand so Señorita Esmeralda could place her hand on his arm and be led to the floor.

The orchestra leader announced the paseo. Diego ran through the dances he had learned at home and was sure he had never heard of this one. But the ladies formed a circle in the center, the gentlemen another circle outside. A dim picture of the geometry came back to Diego. He bowed, his pants didn't split, and the music began. At that instant he noticed the face of the young hidalgo beside him: the tightness, the quivering lips. He saw the same painful fear he felt. *Are we all full of panic?* he asked himself, but the dance had started.

And once again it was a game. Once again—perhaps because the perfect face of Esmeralda reappeared as the dancers' circles revolved and met—it was fun. He discovered that being naturally athletic helped.

The dance ended. Against all expectation, Diego was sorry. His face was red and eager. He wanted to reach for Esmeralda's hand and linger on the dance floor. Instead, he hid his happiness and held out his arm to lead her back to the crowd.

They walked a few paces. She looked at him with expectation. Diego realized with a start that he was expected to say something. *What?* he said to himself. *I don't know what to say! This is the trouble with having a brother who doesn't speak!*

Diego shouted to his brain, *Say something . . . good!*

"You . . . ," he began, and she looked more carefully at him, waiting. "You dance like a crane."

She blossomed into laughter, high and delicate. Her fan hid her smile for a moment. "Are you telling me, Don Diego, that I dance like a long-legged bird?" She laughed again.

"No, no! I mean, yes! You do. But have you ever seen

cranes dance? Have you seen them dance for each other in the spring on the marshes? It's beautiful. Marvelous. They lack only the music."

She thought a moment. "No, Don Diego, I have never seen cranes dance. Until I do, I will presume that I have received a compliment."

At this moment Diego's worst fears came true. He tripped over his own feet and fell onto the floor like a sack of corncobs.

On the floor Diego noticed an embroidered boot being quickly withdrawn. He hadn't tripped over his own feet, but over the cleverly placed foot of Rafael Moncada.

15

A SPECIAL DANCE

IEGO WAS TOO MUCH of an athlete to hurt himself in a little fall. But his ribs ached from a pocket full of almonds he had stashed there for the ride to the hacienda. There was startled silence. He had to recover some shred of dignity! He had one of his sudden ideas.

He rolled onto his back and in the same movement threw his legs in a tuck toward his head. On his roll he hid a handful of almonds in his palm. With the rolling momentum he landed on his boots and bobbed up like a comical child's toy. There were a few titters of surprise. But he didn't stop there.

Whipping out his silk kerchief, he bent over Rafael Moncada's fancy boot. "Rafael! How stupid, how clumsy, how inexcusably rude I've been! I stepped on your boot, poor thing!" He whacked at the fancy boot as if it had all the trail dust of the drag on it.

"Stop that!" Rafael said testily.

"Let me assure myself that it isn't scuffed or torn!" Diego looked up with a particularly sweet smile and said, "I think it will still hold your foot."

Rafael began to sputter, but Diego said, "And every wind blows a little good. See? I've retrieved your nut where you dropped it when I cruelly injured you." He held up the almond. "But it's too soiled for a fine hidalgo." He popped it into his mouth. "Delicious," he said. "I compliment you."

"I wasn't eating nuts!"

"But of course you were, my dear Rafael! See?" He reached to Rafael's coat lapel and seemed to pluck an almond from behind it. It was White Owl's simple trick again.

"Dear Rafael," he said, "they are tasty. But has your grandmother never told you 'Don't put nuts in your ears'?" He plucked a nut from Rafael's left ear, then his right ear, and popped both in his mouth.

"Mm! Even more serious: never, never put nuts in your nose!" He plucked an almond from Rafael's nose and was about to pop it into his mouth but made a little face and said, "Excuse me, but I don't think I'll eat this one."

Everyone around them was laughing. Esmeralda's laugh was especially delightful to Diego.

Rafael was seething with anger. "Shut up, fool! You have no right to shame the house of Moncada!" Rafael had a tendency to spit a little when he was shouting. It was not a pretty thing.

Diego put his hand to his head in a show of distress. "No! I've stepped on you and now I've shamed you! How can I bear the grief?"

More laughter from the circle of guests. This made Rafael even angrier. He spluttered before shouting at Diego, "Insolent puppy! Clown! Play your tricks on Indians in the hills and pay some respect to your betters!"

Diego looked around him with a worried expression. "My betters? My betters? If I can find them, I'll certainly do my best." More laughter.

Rafael was now so angry that he couldn't control himself. "You'll find out soon enough, you stinking peasant. The Moncadas will rule their own kingdom without half-breeds like you in their way! The day is coming when—"

Don Miguel Moncada's hand came down hard on his son's shoulder. "Rafael!" he boomed in his most charming voice. "You are overexcited, my boy. Contain yourself." The room had gone silent.

Diego's eyes were sharp on Rafael's face. What had he said about a kingdom?

"This filthy Indian . . . ," Rafael hissed, though his father's hand was tight on his shoulder.

One of the many extraordinary things about Don Alejandro was that his soft, pleasing voice could cut through a crowd with enormous authority. "Rafael," he said, not loudly, but in the hush it sounded like a trumpet. He came to the edge of the circle. "Rafael, perhaps you will explain yourself."

Señor Moncada's white-knuckled hand turned the reluctant Rafael toward Don Alejandro. The hand shook him slightly, and the boy blurted, "I meant nothing by it."

"I grant you, young Moncada, that my foolish son is often filthy." The don looked about to the guests and said, "Young boys are generally filthy creatures. It is their nature." A few laughed nervously, and he continued to Rafael, "But you may wish to explain how his Indian blood and your"—a small smile came to his lips—"more refined blood affect us here in this room. Many of our families take pride in their connection to those who lived here before us."

141

He raised his hand and brought Doña Regina up beside him. She made a graceful curtsy, surely the most beautiful woman in the room. Her expression was mocking, confident—a strong woman who placed herself second to no one.

Rafael opened and closed his mouth. His father's hand tightened even more on his shoulder. "I meant nothing at all. . . ."

"I'm sure you did not," Don Alejandro said, "for a true gentleman would never give such an insult. I'm sure you have an interesting view about what you've said. Perhaps we can discuss it another time, in another place." These were dangerous, pointed words to Rafael Moncada. He stood on the polite but sharp edge of a duel, and no one in the pueblo was foolish enough to cross swords with Don Alejandro.

"I beg your pardon, Señor. I have offended you without meaning to."

Don Alejandro bowed his acceptance of this apology.

Rafael then bowed to the circle of hidalgos and rushed away. He headed toward a side room where the coats were hung.

Rafael was still shaking with rage and relief. He had been humiliated. If Don Alejandro had insisted on a duel, he would have been close to death. He walked on rubbery legs toward the cloakroom, happy to have some simple thing to do. His anger was just beginning to surface again. He seized the wrought iron handle of the door and tore it open to get—

A grizzly bear! Huge! Fur bristling, teeth like daggers, shaking and letting go a terrible roar!

Rafael spun and ran back into the courtyard. "Aaaaaah!" he shrieked. "Help! Help! Bear! Big! Help!" He could hear the bear's awful feet pattering on the stones behind him. He had one object, the fig tree in the center of the courtyard. The guests parted like curtains. He was almost there!

He caught the toe of his embroidered boot on a stone's edge and fell forward!

The bear roared again.

Rafael couldn't waste the time to leap up. He ran toward the tree on his hands and knees, like his aunt's lap dog rushing toward a meal.

Roar!

Rafael Moncada swarmed up the fig tree like a squirrel, up into the topmost branches, hooting all the way and calling, "Help! Help!"

Why didn't anyone help him? Why were they laughing? Why was the orchestra starting again?

He looked back down for the first time. There was something strange about the bear. Its back legs were white. Its front legs had buttoned seams. It was dancing!

One, two, three, kick to the side! One, two, three, kick to the other side!

Under the tanned bearskin, Diego and Bernardo were dancing a children's dance to an old country tune. They danced around the tree to the enormous laughter of the crowd.

There was applause; glasses were lifted to them.

"That Moncada boy must have been in on the joke. Look at him up there, pretending to be frightened. No one could shriek like that and mean it."

One, two, three, kick! One, two, three, kick!

To the crowd's applause, Diego and Bernardo danced out of the courtyard, waving their floppy bearskin arms behind them.

Like any good ball, the celebration lasted all night. Diego returned to dance with Esmeralda, his mother, and many others. Bernardo returned to thank the orchestra leader and to play his flute. Don Alejandro was a grand figure on the dance floor. Big gatherings were not Regina's favorite events, but she endured them with a grace and dignity that some hidalgos interpreted as aloofness. Rafael Moncada returned, pretending to be part of the joke, but he retired early.

In the gray first light, the de la Vegas and their vaquero escort rode north and west toward their hacienda.

Diego and Bernardo were happily tired, riding behind, letting their horses follow the others, almost dozing at times.

Don Alejandro reined his stallion and fell back with them. They rode a mile or so in companionable silence before he said to Diego, "Do you remember being bitten by a rattlesnake?"

Both boys immediately crossed themselves. "*Sí, Papá.* It was horrible!"

"How did you get the rattlesnake to bite you?"

"The rattler doesn't want to bite," Diego said. "But if you put it in a corner and force it to fight, it will use its fangs." He shuddered a little, remembering the pain and fever he had endured at the end of his vision quest. He came close to dying in the forest, but was saved by Bernardo.

The don nodded. "Never corner a rattlesnake. With men, try to leave even the most offensive man a way to escape with some honor. Corner a man and deny him

145

his honor, and he'll bite."

Bernardo nodded and looked back toward the Honorio hacienda.

"That's right, Bernardo. You boys have made a serious enemy. He's now more than annoying. He'll do anything to hurt you. Don Miguel Moncada is a man of touchy honor as well. He may see your prank as an attack on his name. You denied Rafael a way to retreat with honor."

"But—" Diego began.

Don Alejandro held up his hand. "I'm not saying he didn't deserve to be knocked down a bit. He's a nasty bit of business, young Moncada. And I'm not saying that either of you would hold a grudge if someone played the same trick on you. I know you both too well: you'd be angry, and then you'd laugh your heads off."

The boys smiled.

"But the Moncadas have a thorn in their thumb about something. Perhaps something to do with the mother and her . . . circumstances."

"I thought she had died," Diego said.

Don Alejandro shook his head no. The boys looked interested, but the don was not going to gossip for them.

"Whatever the reason, they will go to greater lengths to ensure their honor than others might. Who knows? Perhaps I am wrong. But I want my boys to keep themselves safe. Beware, yes?"

"*Sí, Papá*," Diego said, and Bernardo nodded.

"This may be of no consequence. Rafael travels to Barcelona this year for his schooling. He may not survive the experience. There are many honor-crazy young blades there, and they back it up with steel. If he matures, he may come back to us a changed man. God bless him."

They crossed themselves and rode on in the first flash of the morning sun over the mountains.

16

THE POPPY BRAND

THE FIESTA WAS OVER for this year. There were dozens of stories to last until the next fiesta. They would circulate up and down the coast with travelers on the Camino Real and on the coastal boats. In San Diego and Acapulco and Panama, they would tell about the grizzly bear that had visited the ball at the Honorio hacienda and danced its way into the night.

The vaqueros had almost recovered from the sleepless nights of dancing and singing, too much wine and food, the easy life. They would grumble about returning to hard riding, but it was really what they did well, what they loved. Once a year they were obliged to stop riding for a few days and teach the townsfolk how to celebrate properly. Then it was time to mount up again.

Other ranchos would begin tanning and making tallow later, when the official Spanish trade boats came up the coast. The de la Vega rancho had its secret agreement with Captain Carter and the *Two Brothers*. Don Alejandro began the work immediately.

Butchers and tanners from the mission, the pueblo, and other ranchos moved into tents and de la Vega barns. Firewood was cut, hearths were set up, and the great cauldrons stood ready. New tanning pits were dug and lined. The big two-wheeled carts were repaired for the heavy hauling to come. The vaqueros began to single out the cattle.

It was a big, ugly business. No one could enjoy it. The best they could do was to be skillful and quick.

Diego and Bernardo walked beside Scar, watching one of the first cattle go through the process. A bull was cut from the herd and driven into a chute of woven saplings and branches. Alone in the chute, it was killed with one hard blow from an ax. It was dragged a few paces, and the skinning began. A pair of tanners working with short, quick strokes took the whole hide in one ragged piece, up to the ears and down to the ankles. Other tanners laid it hair-side down on smooth logs and scraped the fat and flesh into big tubs. The scraped hides were slid into the tanning pits, flooded

149

dark brown with preserving oak bark.

The boys stepped back as the grisly carcass was swung up to the branch of a tree for butchering. With the first cut, the guts came tumbling out. Women picked through them briefly for a few delicacies—parts of the stomachs made tripe for *menudo* soup; the kidneys and sweetbreads went for other dishes. Creamy slabs of fat went into tubs. The rest went into barrels to be hauled off to one of the *arroyos de la muerte*, the ravines of death where bears, wolves, coyotes, wild boar, and scavengers prospered on the leavings.

Diego gagged a bit. The smell was awful.

"The smell of death," Scar said. "The smell of every butchery and battlefield. We are brothers of the cattle. The smell is the same."

Diego shook his head, both disgusted and fascinated by the intricate, intensely colorful insides of the bull.

Bernardo drew his hand across his throat: This big process, all death.

Scar nodded. "Cattle die; the pueblo lives. The cattle live a few easy years, grazing and resting, and they come to this. We accept their death, use their bodies, and make our living from them. It's too easy to think of this sentimentally, as if it were a wicked thing."

"What's the way to think about it?" Diego asked.

"Gratefully," Scar said simply. He motioned toward a cart filling up with barrels of guts and bones. "That's a trip we all make. All of us, to the *arroyo de la muerte*. We have longer than the cattle do. We can be grateful for that. And we can be grateful for the cattle's help."

The butchers worked the big carcasses quickly, separating the cuts of beef with long, curved knives as sharp as razors. The big roasts and joints of beef had their fat trimmed into the tubs and were dropped into tight barrels of scalding, strong brine. The barrels would be sold to ships as "salt horse," beef preserved in strong brine that would keep for years.

Other butchers at tables cut beef into thin strips, casting them into barrels of water, wine, and spices. When the strips had marinated in their flavorings, women would hang them on racks over smoky fires to dry as jerky. Some would be eaten in the saddle or on the trail. Some would be beaten and ground by Estafina into rich, spicy winter dishes. Some of the jerky would be sold in cloth bags to ships.

Carts returning from the *arroyo de la muerte* brought more firewood. Scar and the boys followed the fat tubs to the long line of fires under iron cauldrons. The smell here was meaty and rich.

"They look like hell's demons," Diego said.

Working in the smoke near the flames, smut-soiled neophytes from the mission swung long-handled pitchforks to drop fat, meat, and big bones into the boiling water. Several times an hour, the cauldron was skimmed for fat, which was ladled into a copper cooling vat. Thick and whitish-gray, this tallow was poured into hide leather bags, each weighing half as much as a man.

Hides and tallow, the riches of the pueblo. The *Two Brothers* would trade them somewhere on the rim of the Pacific Ocean for gold and trade goods. The hides would be used for leather goods, belting for the new steam engines, shoes, harness, and saddles. The tallow would be turned into candles to light homes and burn on church altars.

When they saddled up, Diego looked back and said, "We need all those skills to make the pueblo work. Butchers, tanners, herders, candlemakers, barrel makers . . ."

Scar nodded. "Cattle and skills are being stolen. If too many are taken, the pueblo will shrivel up like an unwatered vine. Someone's greed could kill us."

Diego fell behind Bernardo as they rode along a narrow ravine trail. Scar had sent them to tell Juan Three-fingers and his crew that more cattle were needed at the rancho's hide and tallow works.

They broke out of the trees into a meadow. A dozen crows and a few vultures flew up. Diego's blood chilled for a moment, remembering Señor Porcana's body. They reined in their ponies and explored the steep sides of the ravine.

This time it was only a dead cow. "Saints and cats and little kittens," Diego said, "I couldn't have taken another murder."

Bernardo signed to Diego: I was afraid of the same thing.

The cow had fallen over an embankment above the ravine. The tumble through trees had broken its neck. They had watched many skinnings by now. It was a chore, but it had to be done.

Diego stepped across the body to attach his reata. "It's a Moncada cow," he called to Bernardo. "Here's the poppy brand. Why did Moncada make his mark so complicated? It looks more like a wrought-iron fence than a cattle brand."

Bernardo flounced his fingers under his chin, like a ruffled shirt collar. It was one of their signs for "over-dressed" or "showy."

"Don Moncada is showy, that's for sure. He dresses like a peacock."

Bernardo held up two fingers.

"Yes, Rafael Moncada is a dandy, too. When he comes back from Barcelona, he'll be unbearable. A new outfit every day." Diego laughed. "He might even come back wearing dresses."

He remounted and backed his pony. The cow slid out of the trees. At the edge of the meadow, they tied off their horses, unsaddled them, and took off their shirts for the messy work. Range law was clear: the branded cow was Moncado property. They would skin the cow and send the hide to the Moncada rancho. The meat was of no importance out here.

They pulled the knives from their boots and began. Diego started with a necklace cut around the neck. From that, he ran a long cut along the belly. Bernardo cut around the ankles, then up the legs toward the belly cut. They worked under the sun in the friendly silence of brothers.

They rolled the carcass one way, separating the hide from the cow's left side down to the backbone. Then they rolled it the other way to slice away the right side.

Bernardo rattled the back of his knife against his spur, calling attention to something. Diego looked back from his work on the forward part. "What?"

He pointed with his knife point to the scarred flesh under the brand.

"Yes, that's the trouble with a big, showy brand. A lot of scarring."

Bernardo pulled Diego closer: Look!

He flipped the hide down and lifted it up. Again: down and up. He pointed at the center of the scarring.

It took a full minute for Diego to see it. "Yes! The fresh scars are only for part of the brand! Some of this brand was made last year or the year before. Some was made just this spring."

Bernardo flipped the hide down again, and they looked at the brand. Diego ran his knife point along two lines within the complicated symbol. He looked under the hide again. No fresh scars appeared for those two lines. They met at a sharp angle to make the big de la Vega *V*.

Bernardo held two fingers up in a *V*.

"St. Bernard's bees!" Diego said softly. This was awful. Here was evidence of deception and a huge theft. Or was it?

"Is this what I think it is?" Diego asked Bernardo.

Bernardo shrugged and beckoned with two fingers: I don't know; tell me what you think it is.

"Moncada has had his men changing brands.

They've re-branded de la Vega *V*'s as Moncada poppy brands. Maybe hundreds of them. The hundreds we're missing!"

Bernardo traced another possible path in the complicated brand: a *G* and a cross.

"They could have changed the mission's brand, too! There's Mission San Gabriel's *G* and the cross!"

Bernardo stamped his boot: Why didn't we think of this before?

"We didn't think of it because no one in the pueblo ever needed to steal cattle! Indians from the hills might slaughter one or two head for food, but they always left the hides, the valuable parts. The *apartado* has always separated the herds fairly."

Bernardo poked at the brand angrily.

"True, the *apartado* separated them by brands. They used the brands!"

Bernardo's face was dark with anger.

"Why would Moncada need to change the brands? He's a wealthy hidalgo. Why does he need more?"

They stared at the hide, as if it would speak to them. In a way it did. Diego shot up and walked around the carcass in a circle. "It begins to come together, Bernardo. You were getting the bearskin ready, and I was playing tricks with Rafael. He was so angry that I think he said something he shouldn't have. He said 'The Moncadas will rule their own kingdom without half-breed peasants like you in their way!' His father shut him up, stopped him immediately. I think the Moncadas are planning their own kingdom."

Bernardo shook his head: That's crazy!

"Yes, it's almost more than I can possibly believe. But what else is there? Could Don Moncada be stealing the pueblo's men for this kingdom? Is he financing a Moncada kingdom with stolen cattle? Is he that vicious? That ambitious?"

The boys looked at the bloody carcass of the cow at their feet. Both of them wished they'd never seen it. This darkness came too close to their lives.

17

BOATS IN THE NIGHT

THEY STOOD IN THE stable yard without speaking. Don Alejandro was calm and thoughtful. Scar showed his smoldering anger. Bernardo was even more withdrawn than usual. Diego had done his talking and, for once, had nothing more to say.

The fresh, bloody hide hung over a fence rail before them. It was the evidence of a crime committed by an *Angeleño*, one of their own. A man they trusted and respected had cheated the pueblo. The loss of the cattle was bearable, no more than an annoyance. But the loss of trust was staggering. They could no longer do business in an easy, careless way. Because of Moncada, life in Pueblo de los Angeles would be tighter and more suspicious. This was the real damage.

Don Alejandro shook his head. "We know the truth

for ourselves now. Officially, legally, we know nothing. This one hide? Moncada can deny he had anything to do with it. He can blame it on anyone, even on us. And who will skin out all the Moncada cattle and examine all the brands? Impossible."

"*Papá,* here is the question Bernardo and I have been asking ourselves: Why has Moncada tried to increase his herds like this? Remember you said that perhaps the skilled men were being kidnapped because someone wanted to start a colony? We think Moncada is trying to finance his own kingdom with cattle—our cattle, mission cattle, everyone else's cattle. And he is stealing our men to make his kingdom run."

"That's a long stretch of logic, Diego. How do you connect the two?"

"At the ball Rafael Moncada told me that the Moncadas would soon rule their own lands."

"Rafael's a boy, a foolish boy."

"Even so, when he said it his father almost leaped to shut him up."

The don considered this for a time. "You may have struck on the truth, boys. Moncada may well be the mind and will behind this evil. But to stop him, I must have something more substantial. I must bring evidence to the *ayuntamiento,* the council of hidalgos. They will not want to believe that one of their own is this treacherous. Rafael's bragging isn't enough to prove the case. I don't think the hidalgos would accept that Don Miguel Moncada was involved in kidnapping and murder."

"Then let's bring him to justice for stealing cattle and see what he says!" Diego said.

Don Alejandro held up his hand. "We may be able to discourage him from changing brands. Letting him know we suspect something is enough to do that. But to punish him? Spanish courts are no nearer than Mexico City. You know we can't trust the *comandante's* frail ethics. We've seen how Moncada manipulates him. He uses what few soldiers the pueblo has like Moncada's personal troops. No, Moncada won't be punished for the brands."

"But where's the justice in that?"

Don Alejandro's laugh was short and bitter. "Justice, caballeros, is not a fixed star. It wanders and changes. Remember this, Diego: Nothing is as important or as elusive as justice. It is a rare thing, even in the courts of law. Seize it where you can, when you can. In Spain or even France, the courts might be reliable. In Pueblo de los Angeles, we have a handful of drunken troopers and a corrupt *comandante*, while the official packet carrying mail hasn't arrived for months. Today justice escapes us."

The don turned away from the hide. "There is something you boys don't know yet. Estafina's husband, Montez, is missing. I sent him to the pueblo for a load of tanbark. We found the wagon empty, but he never came back. He's our best tanner, a fine leather worker. Estafina will be crushed."

Diego was stunned by the news. Montez! He was a man as familiar and kind as the warmth of Estafina's kitchen. How could anyone take Montez away?

Bernardo was not stunned. He was coldly, dangerously angry. The thought of Montez kidnapped echoed the pain of his mother taken from him.

Don Alejandro continued, "I agree with you. I think Moncada is behind this. I'd like to hoist him on my sword point within the hour. Would that bring Montez and our men back? No. This thing is a giant knot of evil. We must patiently undo its strands, one by one."

He spun back and struck the hide with his riding quirt as if he were striking Moncada. "And this thing, this shameful thing . . . keep it in our storeroom until we have solid evidence to go with it."

Scar nodded and spat in the dust of the stable yard.

"Now, *hijos*, grieved or not, we still have the business

of a rancho to do. Do me the kindness to ride to San Pedro and ask if there is any word of the *Two Brothers*. We will unravel this mystery, but we must also think about sending our hides and tallow to sea."

The boys saddled two good mares for the ride to San Pedro. They led them out into the stable yard, ready to mount up. Regina called to them from the walled herb garden.

They found her with Stands Stooped, talking as two old friends might talk in White Owl's village. Both were squatting on their heels, backs against the stucco wall. It was a little strange that one wore deerskin leggings and the other wore a silk dress pulled up around her knees. Regina led two separate lives—she was both Gabrieleño and hidalgo. Sometimes they overlapped.

"Our brother Stands Stooped has a message from Trout Spot," she said.

Stands Stooped nodded as Diego and Bernardo squatted beside them. "You asked the *tomyaar* to track any clues to this slavery mystery," he said. "We've heard nothing unusual from our brothers in the mountains, and nothing from our brothers along the routes north and south. But there are some strange signs from our coast brothers. The fishing people have seen boats coming and going from the first big Channel Island in the north, the one you call Santa Cruz. They are seen only at night, putting off from the mainland beach and not from San Pedro Harbor. Very secret. White sailors have set up a camp on the other side of the island. There is a big ship anchored out there in the channel between the islands. They will not allow the fishing people anywhere near their camp. For me, anything white sailors do is suspicious. But Trout Spot and White Owl are wiser than I am, and they are suspicious too."

He stopped, picked up a handful of dirt, and cast it down, as if to say, "There it is."

All four of them nodded. Regina clasped Stands Stooped by the arm. "Good information, brother," she said.

"We will find out more about this," Diego said in the Shoshone tongue. "Give our thanks to Trout Spot for his vigilance. He is a wise friend."

"Your evil is our evil," Stands Stooped said simply. He stirred to rise and go, but Regina put her hand on his shoulder.

"Stay and eat with us, brother. You have a long journey."

Diego said, "With apologies, we won't eat with you. *Papá* has asked us to ride to San Pedro for news of the ship *Two Brothers.* Now that I've heard this message, I'm thinking that friends in San Pedro may know something about these secret boat trips. Will you tell *Papá* that we'll be back as soon as we can?"

She looked at them for a long moment. She was troubled by what might harm her boys.

Stands Stooped said softly, "They're boys. But they're men, too. They have brave blood, Toypurnia, and they'll be strong."

Regina nodded, her mouth set. "Take care, my young *Californios,* and *vayan con Dios.*"

Trinidad ran along the dock, happy to see them. "I didn't see you at all during the fiesta," she chirped. "The fishing has been great this week! You should have been here! Why the sad faces? What are you up to down here? It's too late for day fishing, but we might catch some sprats along the beach with a net. I'll get the net, but those boots and spurs—"

"Trinidad!" Diego stopped her. "We can't fish. There are serious things going on."

"So that's why you two are looking so downcast. Old Bernie here looks like a flounder." She punched his shoulder, trying to cheer him up.

"Listen for a moment, at least! Is Stackpole here?

164

Can we all talk together?"

"He's in the shack making dinner. Have you eaten? Fish and rice, plenty for all of us. You like fish and rice?" She was a fountain of words, constantly bubbling.

At the table Stackpole laid tin plates and dished out food.

Diego was distracted. He couldn't even think of eating. "Something that could be very bad is happening out on the islands," he began.

"Diego and Bernie are long faced about something," Trinidad crowed. "Faces as sour as lemons. No time for fishing, no time for—"

Stackpole leaned across the little table. "Trinidad, if you don't close your mouth, I am going to hit you with this frying pan."

"No need to be prickly about it. All you had to do was ask." She sulked.

"Quiet!" Stackpole said. "That's an order! Diego, tell me what's happening."

Diego paused, wondering if Trinidad would say anything more, but she looked up at the ceiling as if she wasn't concerned with words. He began, "You know that dozens of skilled men have disappeared from the pueblo. Captain Carter lost his barrel maker too."

165

Stackpole nodded. "Our friend Montez, our best tanner, has disappeared as well. Don Alejandro believes someone is kidnapping skilled men to set up a new colony."

"Maybe," Stackpole said, and he rolled the idea around in his mind.

"The pueblo's potter, Señor Porcana, was kidnapped and then killed trying to escape. We found his body."

Trinidad wasn't gazing at the ceiling now. She chewed her fish with all her attention focused on Diego.

"We heard from . . . someone, a truthful person"— Diego didn't want to mention El Chollo's name— "that outside riders killed Porcana. The same riders must have kidnapped the others. Tough men paid by someone to grab them and take them away."

Stackpole shook his head, putting the frying pan aside. "This is more serious than I thought. This must be a slaving gang. I hadn't heard of any blackbirders on this coast but—"

Bernardo tapped the table, looked at Diego, and nodded toward the pueblo.

"Yes!" Diego turned to Stackpole. "Did you just use the word 'blackbirders'?"

Stackpole nodded. "The worst kind of men. That's

what they call men who ship black slaves from Africa to the Caribbean and then up to the States. A vile trade. The ships are packed so tightly that they lose a third, sometimes half, of the slaves coming across."

"We got into a scrape with a bunch of sailors in the pueblo before the fiesta," Diego said excitedly. "They said they were blackbirders and had shipped black men between Africa and Jamaica. They were a rough bunch."

"They would be. You'd never get your soul clean if you ever shipped with blackbirders."

Diego thought a moment. "This makes more and more sense. Tough foreign vaqueros. Blackbirders in the pueblo. We got word through our Gabrieleño friends that the fishing Indians have seen boats putting off the beach at night. They head for Santa Cruz. Someone has a big ship anchored on the far side of the island, off a camp of some sort. They don't allow anyone near it."

Stackpole nodded. "That would be about right. They'd need riders ashore to capture slaves. And they'd have a camp to gather a full load before they shoved off for . . . wherever they were going. I'll tell you this, though: once they shove off, you'd never see your friends again. Ever. They'd be taken to someplace so far away they couldn't return. Slavers don't accept the possibility of return. It's a long way from the southern States to Africa. No one goes back."

"How could we find out about this camp?" Diego asked.

Stackpole looked at a chart pinned to the wall of the shack. "Just sailing up to it would do more harm than good. You might get them jumpy enough to leave immediately."

"I don't see a problem," Trinidad said around a mouthful of fish and rice.

Diego erupted, "No problem? What are you talking about? This is—"

"It's easy," she said. "Look!" She jumped up and pointed to the east coast of the big island on the chart. "I've landed here a hundred times. I could do it in the dark. We land here, climb over the ridge, and come down behind the camp as quiet as mice. We'd see everything. Where's the problem?"

"That's ridiculous!" Diego said. "They'd see you coming a mile away!"

Stackpole traced the island shoreline on the chart with his finger. "She may be right," he said.

"Ha! Ha, Mr. Fancy Hidalgo Vaquero!" she crowed.

"But she's right about another thing. You'd be forced to do it at night. You wouldn't want one of their lookouts on the point here seeing you coming." He pointed to the tip of Santa Cruz.

"When could we do it?" Diego asked.

"Tonight," Trinidad said. "Why not tonight? The breeze is right. It's running right up the channel, which is rare enough. We've still got a few hours before sunset. We could make it there tonight."

"You'd catch the tide," Stackpole said. He took down an almanac and leafed to a page. "You'd have a quarter moon rising two hours after sundown. Enough to see by, but it would be hard to spot a little boat at a distance. I hate to say it, but tonight might be best."

Diego looked at Bernardo. They nodded at each other.

"I'm going with you," Stackpole said.

Diego shook his head. "No, *Capitán*. With respect, you should stay behind to tell someone we went. If we don't come back tomorrow, someone should come for us."

Stackpole nodded. "No one can get you there better than Trinidad. She knows the currents and the rocks better than anyone"—the girl grinned with pride— "and she can handle that little boat better than anyone."

"Let's get this straight, Diego," Trinidad said with a

smirk. "On the water, I'm the captain. It's me who's in charge. Got that?"

Diego sighed; Bernardo shrugged.

Stackpole laughed. "Her big revenge. She gets to order you two around. Well, at least she'll bother someone other than me for a change. I'll get you some heavy sweaters. The wind's chilly out there."

—⚬ 18 ⚬—

THE ISLAND CAMP

THE NIGHT WAS AS black as pitch from the tar pits. The only light was a tiny candle shaded in the compass box at Trinidad's feet. In the bit of reflected glow, her face was easy, untroubled. She watched the compass, then the stars, then the black shape of the sail against the stars. Her head nodded between them, up and down. Her hand on the tiller shifted only a little this way, a little that way. The big Pacific swell lifted under the tiny boat and dropped away so the motion was a long, easy swoop. Bubbles caught in the bow wave passed under the hull and hissed away from the transom. Water gurgled musically inside the centerboard box. Trinidad hummed softly to herself with her watching rhythm: compass, stars, sail, compass, stars, sail.

Diego and Bernardo sat against the windward rail of the boat. They were wrapped in a spare sail for warmth. Diego knew he should be afraid: he didn't know what they were sailing into, and they were out on the colossal Pacific in a boat as big as the hacienda's dining table. Yet there sat Trinidad, as calm as Estafina making tortillas in the morning. The boat's motion had a comforting regularity. He felt the lift and fall of the sea, and somehow felt the pressure of the wind in the sail. He felt the driving rush of the boat, too, purposeful and sure.

Diego thought Trinidad would be chatty and annoying for the entire trip. But out here she was another person.

Fans and frilled dresses? Not this tough little woman. Diego remembered the blacksmith's daughter fleeing in tears from the blackbirders. He was glad Trinidad hadn't been there. If a blackbirder had asked her to sit on his lap, there would have been broken crockery flying and something like a bull-and-bear fight. Trinidad would have gotten them into even more trouble. But he liked her for that.

It was Diego who broke the silence. "Are you warm enough?"

"Hm?" Her humming stopped. "Oh, sure. Thick

sweater. Stackpole made it."

"Knitted it?"

"Sure. Great knitter, Stackpole. Black sheep's wool, unwashed. Oil still in it. Sailor stuff." Then she fell back to humming, and the conversation was over.

Against all expectations, Diego slumped against Bernardo and the two boys slept like babies in a rocking cradle, wrapped in a canvas blanket. In the rhythm of the boat's motion, Diego dreamed about dancing with Esmeralda Avila.

"What?" Diego jerked awake, unsure of where he was for a moment. Trinidad had touched his arm. The motion of the boat had changed in some way, and the light of the risen moon made everything remarkably bright.

"Diego. Bernie. We're about half a mile from shore here, so pay attention." Her voice was soft. "Don't shout; don't talk out loud. Voices carry over water. When we get close to shore, things will happen quickly. You want to be ready and know what to do."

"What do we do?" Diego asked. His vanity was stung, because this was all unfamiliar to him and a red-headed girl was firmly in charge.

"Simple," she said. "We'll be coming into a little

stretch of sand beach behind a big rock. When I tell you to get ready, Diego, you get to the starboard side of the bow. That's your right side. Bernardo, you stay on the port side, where you are now. I'll bring down the sail, and we'll come in slowly. When I say, 'Now,' both of you jump out on your sides and hold onto the boat. We'll be in water maybe up to your waist. If it's deeper, don't panic. You'll feel the bottom quick enough."

"So we stand on the bottom?" he asked.

"Don't stand there, but grab the edge of the boat and run up the beach with it as far as you can drag it with the wave. Okay?"

"We jump out, grab the boat, and drag it up the beach. Why aren't you jumping out?"

"Because I'm the captain."

"That's no good reason!" Diego hissed.

"I'm kidding," she said quietly. "I stay here to keep weight in the stern so the bow is light and rides up on the beach. I'll be in the water as soon as it grounds out."

"Oh," Diego said, telling himself he should have thought of that. Well, how good would she be roping a bull?

"You want to grab that painter, too?"

"What painter? Why do we have to paint?"

174

"No. The painter is what we call the line that's attached to the bow."

"Why don't you just call it—"

"Hush," she said, "we're getting close now. Are you ready?"

The boys nodded.

She stood for a moment and gathered the sail as it came down, tucking it into a roll. She sat down again. "Ready?"

Bernardo and Diego nodded. A house-sized rock was looming over them.

The boat paused on the crest of a wave, then rushed forward. "Now!" Trinidad called over the wave's roar.

Diego vaulted over the bow and plunged into the water up to his waist. The bottom was hard sand. The boat that had seemed so small tugged at him like a cow pony. His legs were slow in the water as he pulled up toward the beach. He heard Trinidad plunge over the stern and felt her push forward. It touched once, twice, then the wave fell back and they were out of the water.

"Here comes another wave," Trinidad whispered. "Keep pulling!"

When the second wave fell back, the boat sat solidly in the sand. Trinidad took the painter from Diego and ran up the beach, tying it around a boulder.

"See that rock face above us?" she whispered. "There's a trail along its base. It reaches over that way, then switches back a few times before the ridge. Off to the right, along the ridge, there's a trail leading down to the beach on the far side. It may be hard to find in the dark."

The boys followed Trinidad, plunging into shadows. They stumbled at first, following more by sound than sight, but their eyes sharpened even in the dim light. They mounted the steep slope at an angle.

Diego was aware of a vertical wall on one side. They had reached the trail along the rock face. They changed directions several times with the trail. He was glad Trinidad knew her way. He would have been lost long before.

They stopped on the ridge, breathing heavily. Bernardo clicked his tongue like an insect and pointed down. The lights of a few fires glimmered through the trees below.

"If you have a trumpet," Diego whispered, "now is not the time to practice blowing it."

Trinidad did not think this was funny in the least.

When they were several hundred paces along the ridge, Trinidad held up her hand. "Stay here," she said softly. She disappeared and returned. "I found the trail, about fifty paces farther on. It's steep and it's rocky. Take it slow; pick your steps. We don't want any rocks rattling down ahead of us. Are you all set?"

The descent was a nightmare. The darkness was deeper on the western side of the ridge, away from the rising moon, and the footing was difficult. The sense of height on the slope was hard to judge, so when they broke out of the brush suddenly, the camp's fires seemed right in their laps. They backed into the brush again.

It was a big camp. The closest fire was really a hundred paces away. They were in a cupped valley, about five hundred paces from the trees down to the beach. Sailors were talking around one of the fires, laughing. They heard the clink of wine bottles on mugs. And they heard a few low moans from a dark shape close to them.

Diego began to make out the structure of this shape, a stockade of lashed palm trunks and driftwood. Could this be where the blackbirders kept their pueblo slaves?

"I'll get closer," Diego whispered. He shook his head. "I don't like it, but we've got to know what's here."

He could feel Bernardo nod more than see him. He lowered himself to creep on his belly.

Trinidad put her hand on his shoulder and whispered, "Be careful, Diego." She tousled his hair for luck. She was a good friend to have in a tight spot.

From his hands and knees, the stockade looked miles away. He moved with almost painful slowness, putting one hand down, then a knee, then another hand . . . a palm frond fell ten paces from him! The crash sounded like a musket shot. But the breeze was blowing, changing its direction. It must have been a sound familiar to the blackbirders in camp, because they continued their drinking and talking.

He crept like the hands of a clock, it seemed, but he was finally up against the palm trunks of the stockade. He could smell unwashed bodies and urine. Another moan two paces away startled him.

Were these blackbirders or captives? There was only one way to tell, though it would be the most dangerous thing he had done all night.

Diego tossed a pebble at the stockade. "Can someone tell me where Padre Mendoza's mule has gone?" he whispered.

There was a sudden stir of bodies. Diego was terrified.

Then a voice whispered back, "Who wants to know?"

Diego gulped. "Diego de la Vega, amigos. Are you in trouble out here?"

"The worst," the voice replied. "Wait a heartbeat, *hijo*, there is a friend of yours who wants a word with you."

There was a pause, more shifting of bodies, and then the familiar voice of Montez almost in his ear, "Estafina didn't send you with any tamales, did she?"

"No, *Tío*." Diego called Montez "uncle" as he would any older man. "But when she finds that you've been lying about on the islands, doing nothing, you'll be in trouble. She'll say, 'There's work to be done, Montez! The night is for sleep; the day is for work!'"

Montez gave a short chuckle.

"She has missed you. We've all missed you. Help is at hand."

"*Gracias a Dios*," Montez whispered. "God be thanked. Can you get us out of here?"

"How many of you are there, *Tío*?"

A whispered conference behind the stockade, then, "Maybe four dozen, Diego. Men of the pueblo and a few sailors. Why are we here? What did we do to these men?"

"All you did was show your skill. Whoever took you wants only skilled men. We think someone plans to set

179

up some kind of colony. They need you to make it prosper. Who took you?"

Diego heard the voice of the carpenter, Paco Pedernales. "Vaqueros, but of a strange kind. Not *Californios*, but perhaps from somewhere below Panama. Then these bad sailors."

"Did they say where they were taking you, *Tío*?"

"Not by name," Paco whispered mournfully. "Someplace far away, across the ocean. Far from California." He sounded frightened by the distance from home.

"How many sailors are keeping you?"

"Not more than fifteen or twenty, but they are well armed. What can you do for us, Diegolito?" Montez asked.

"Now, tonight, nothing. But with God's grace, we'll get back to the mainland by morning. When Don Alejandro and Estafina come for you, I don't envy those sailors."

"God bless you, *hijo*," Montez said.

"And you, *Tío*. But now I must get back to the mainland and see to your rescue. Adios, *hermanos*."

Diego crawled back to the treeline as slowly and carefully as he had come. But now the fate of his *Angeleño* friends rode with him. The journey felt much longer.

Finally Bernardo's hands gripped his arms and pulled him into the bushes.

Trinidad wanted to know everything immediately, whispering, "Well? What's over there? What's the story?"

"They're all in the stockade, all the pueblo men and some sailors."

"Are they tied up? Are they hurt? Are the blackbirders close?"

"Before we have a public meeting about it, Trinidad, can we just get out of the blackbirders' pockets? We must get back to the mainland as quickly as we can."

"I just wanted some information," she hissed.

"I'll tell you everything when we're on the water again. Get us out of here, Captain!"

The mention of her honorary title satisfied her. She tousled his hair again, and they started up the trail behind her.

When they were across the ridge, Diego asked, "Can you land us near our hacienda?"

"If the wind doesn't change, yes. I can drop you off-shore, but I can't land the boat in surf. We shouldn't sail to San Pedro, first? Are things moving that fast?"

"Fast, very fast. You heard what Stackpole said: if the

blackbirders feel threatened, they'll run with whatever prisoners they have. And once they're gone, none of them will ever come back. Don Alejandro must hear of this immediately."

"What can he do?"

"If the don can't do something, no one can."

On the beach they dragged the boat across the sand into the water. They fought the waves, getting the little vessel off the shore and clear of the rock. There was the mainland looming across the moonlit channel. Diego wished he had wings.

~⤳ 19 ⤳~

COUNCIL OF WAR

THE WIND WAS STRONGER, but it had shifted into the northwest. The steeper waves were behind them as they headed south and east. When the breaking crests passed beneath them, the little boat lifted and surged forward. Diego watched Trinidad constantly maneuver, using the tiller and the sail. This was not the dreamy motion that had lulled him to sleep on the way out.

No matter how sweetly the sea might have rocked him, he could never have slept on this passage—not with this responsibility. How could they rescue their friends?

The moonlit shore seemed to approach like a turtle, in slow jerks. Then it leaped out at them, looming fast. Trinidad was fighting big whitecaps close inshore.

"Diego, Bernie, I can't bring the boat too close without breaking its back on the bottom."

Bernardo made a sign. Diego translated it. "He says he's a duck. Easy."

"I'll get you as close as I can. When it's time to go overboard, we'll wait for a lull between waves. I'll give you the signal. I'll take the boat out again and scoot down to San Pedro and Stackpole."

"Not a word to anyone else!" Diego shouted. The inshore waves were noisy now. He looked ahead to the lines of surf that began off the beach. Then he changed his mind and turned back to Trinidad. "The fishermen in San Pedro . . . Stackpole will know who he can trust?"

She nodded: Of course.

"Whatever the don decides, we'll need boats to get men back out to Santa Cruz." Trinidad's face darkened. "Yes, yes, and women," Diego added. Her face brightened again. "Perhaps as soon as tonight. And, God willing, we'll need boats to bring back four dozen *Angeleños*. When can we get back to the island? What will the weather do to us?"

She thought a moment and shouted over the rising noise of the breakers, "This wind will die out in the afternoon. We can use the land breeze this evening. The tide? Not so bad, not so good. It will be a slow passage this evening, but we can make it."

"Then tell Stackpole to have some trustworthy men and boats ready. But it's got to be kept secret! No one, especially Moncada and his vaqueros, can get wind of this. We need surprise!"

"Stackpole's a Boston Yankee. They're good at keeping things to themselves," she shouted. "Now get ready to swim for it. Over you go!"

Diego and Bernardo rolled over the boat's side between crests. The night was chilly enough that the sea felt almost warm for a moment. Then the illusion disappeared and the cold began. They were struggling to ride the big waves in, desperate to stay close to each other. Stackpole's heavy sweaters felt like lead weights when they lifted their arms out of the water to stroke. They touched bottom once, but that was an offshore sandbar. Then they were tumbled forward by a big breaker and came up spluttering.

They looked behind them and waited for a fresh breaker. It gathered offshore and they started to swim inshore as fast as their clothes would let them. They caught the wave, and for a few thrilling moments they bodysurfed down the face of the wave before being tumbled again. They rode another breaker, and another.

185

The last breaker spit them up onto the beach like bundles of old clothes. They tried to rise and run to dry sand, but the undertow sucked them off their legs long enough to be pounded by a following wave.

They stood in the shallows, streaming with water, sand gritting under their clothes.

Bernardo pointed out to sea. Trinidad had gotten her boat out of the breakers and was running down the channel toward San Pedro. He motioned toward the cliffs ahead: Let's go.

The hacienda door was barred, so they climbed in over the sleeping porch. Not a good idea.

They had walked only a few paces when both Don Alejandro and Regina stepped out of the shadows in their nightshirts, each holding a sword at the ready. Estafina appeared in the hallway with a cocked pistol, and Scar called from the veranda, "*Patrón?*"

"It's Diego and Bernardo, Scar," the don called back. "Come in through the front. Estafina, uncock that pistol and unbar the front door." His face was serious as he turned to the boys. "Where have you been? We've all been upset! Worried sick! You can't rattle around like this on your own!" He was angry, but the boys could see that it came out of his concern for them. He didn't wait for answers. "Get out of those clothes. Dry off and come to the kitchen."

Regina said nothing, but Diego caught her glance and saw the gladness in her face. She was relieved they were back.

The kitchen was warm and bright with candles when they came in. Estafina was kneeling by the hearth fire, feeding it kindling and swinging a pot of stew over the flame. Her creed was simple: If there is trouble, fix food.

"Now, Diego. And you, Bernardo. Explain to me how you justify—"

Diego held up his hand. "Forgive me, *Papá*." He kneeled down beside Estafina and put his arm around her. "I have seen Montez. I have talked to him. He is being held captive, but he is well and sends his love."

Her strong face didn't change expression. There was, perhaps, a tiny trembling of her lips. Tears welled in her eyes. She nodded once and turned back to the fire to hide them. She was one reason Diego was proud to have the warrior blood of the Gabrieleño in him.

Later, after explanations and details, they sat at the table as the morning light rose around the hacienda.

"The four dozen prisoners, they are in a stout stockade, yes?" Don Alejandro was going over some of the situation. When Diego nodded, he continued. "There are fifteen or twenty guards, heavily armed. The camp is in a little . . ." He struggled for a description.

"It's something like a ravine, *Papá*. It opens onto the beach where there is a line of trees at the edge of the sand."

The don nodded. "And there is a path that leads down from the ridge, a path you found by coming up the other side of the ridge?"

"We didn't stumble on it, *Papá*. Trinidad knew it well. She knows the island and all the water around it."

"I wish this child, Trinidad, were here. Is she reliable?"

Bernardo put his hand flat on the table: Absolutely.

Diego said, "She is honest and she has courage. She is at home on the water as Scar is in the saddle."

Don Alejandro looked under raised brows to Diego, doubting this. Then to Scar.

Scar lifted his shoulders a finger's width: Let's hope she is.

"Stackpole has faith in her. And Stackpole is a man we can trust," Diego said.

The don thought a moment, then nodded.

"Stackpole says that if these slavers are frightened, they will leave immediately with whatever prisoners they have now. He thinks time is important."

The don looked at Scar and turned back. "I just hope we have enough time."

"I took a risk, *Papá*. I've asked Stackpole to gather several fishermen and their boats, men he can trust, for tonight."

"That was a risk," the don agreed, "but it was sensible. We'll need them. And I agree that time is crucial. We will strike tonight. But I still need to know more about that island. Scar . . ."

The *mayordomo* leaned forward.

"Send for Juan Three-fingers and his crew, and for six other vaqueros who will be good in a fight. Send word for some of our old soldiers—Hermosa, Juarez, Padillo, Verde—"

"I will be with you," Regina announced. It wasn't a question.

"And I." Estafina rose and placed both of her big hands on the table.

Don Alejandro paused, looked at Estafina's hands, and said, "*Está bien*. That's good." He turned to Scar. "Muskets, fifty rounds for each man . . . and woman. Swords for all and pikes for those who want to carry them. Can you fix me a couple of grenades, like in the old days, Esteban?" Scar grinned around the saber cut on his cheek, looking forward to making some grenades.

"And let's get this Trinidad girl up here. And Stackpole. Send a good man to San Pedro with horses to bring them back. I want everyone here by mid-afternoon with all our tools laid out. We need a council of war, my children."

The don addressed them all as his children, but no one was insulted. *Capitán* Alejandro de la Vega was merely reassuming his rank and station as a leader of troops. True, they were irregular troops: an unusual little army of vaqueros, retired soldiers, boys and women, plus a small navy consisting of a one-legged Yankee, the abandoned child of an Acapulco prostitute, and some mestízo fishermen.

The *capitán* lit a cigar with jaunty confidence: with a force like this, the blackbirders didn't have a chance.

Diego and Bernardo looked at each other. Diego had at first thought the rough-talking dock orphan Trinidad would offend his reserved, often argumentative mother. On second thought, however, they were both wildly independent, strong women.

Doña Regina strode out of the hacienda dressed scandalously in men's riding trousers and a black silk blouse. Her hair was pulled back under a black scarf. She took one look at Trinidad clinging to the saddle horn, at her wild, red hair and her mended trousers dusty from the road. She called, "You are Trinidad? Look at the way these brutes have treated you, all the way from San Pedro!" She gave the vaqueros an evil look.

She passed over Stackpole (who had ridden the same distance and with a whalebone leg that didn't fit a stirrup) with "Señor Stackpole. You are welcome."

Then she returned all her attention to Trinidad. "You must excuse them, little sister. They are accustomed to the company of cows, little more. You will come with me now and refresh yourself."

Trinidad nearly fell from the big mare she had ridden. Regina rushed to help her while the boys stood by. Diego was just as happy that she couldn't ride worth a bean. The two women disappeared into the hacienda.

Don Alejandro was impatient to begin his council of war and paced around the table. But Regina believed there were more important things to do. She reappeared with Trinidad only after the girl's hair had been brushed, she had been washed, and was dressed in clean clothes—fresh trousers with a silk blouse. Bernardo recognized his trousers and Diego the shirt.

"We are at your disposal, gentlemen," Regina said, as if the two women had been waiting all along. She took her place at the table, and the men returned to their seats—Stackpole, Scar and his vaqueros, and half a dozen former soldiers who had served under Don Alejandro. They were older men, with gray in their hair but unmistakable iron in their bearing. Estafina stood in her usual place beside the table. On it was a map of Santa Cruz Island.

"*Está bien*," Don Alejandro said. "Can you read a map, child?"

"She's been raised with nautical charts," Stackpole said, but Trinidad held up her hand to him. She would answer for herself.

"Yes, Señor."

"*Bueno*. Here is a map of Santa Cruz Island. Can you show me approximately where the trails you took are located?"

"No, Señor," she said.

Don Alejandro looked at her, surprised.

"I can show you *exactly* where they are located. Here"—she traced a route with her finger from an indent in the southeastern coast of the island to its

192

ridge—"along the ridge, here, then down to this little valley, here."

The don nodded his approval. "And this ridge road, it goes both ways? Do any other trails descend from it to the southwestern side of the island?"

Trinidad nodded. "The ridge road runs out to here. There is a trail to this beach. It also runs farther to the southeast and connects to a trail here that runs down to this beach."

"Excellent," the don said. There were many questions and many comments, and the table went through a big pot of coffee before the don was satisfied.

"Make no mistake," he addressed everyone in the room, "these slavers are evil men. They are outlaws, no better than pirates. I don't want any of you hurt because you offer too much mercy. Be sensible, be hard, leave your pity at home. We've met some of these men before in the pueblo. My impression is that they'll put up a fight to defend their . . . property." The don's face showed his disgust for slavery. "We must assume they have been in a real battle before. But at sea, on their own terms. We have them on land, and we can box them up like rabbits in a pen. They will not have come up against disciplined soldiers, caballeros. I expect them to crumble and run."

He had drawn a rough map of the valley, showing the stockade where the prisoners were kept, the general locations of the tents and fires Diego had described, and the places trails came down from the ridges.

"You men on the beach, remember your fields of fire. Don't fire directly up the valley, but across it at an angle. We don't want to hit our captive *Angeleños* with bullets meant to free them."

The men nodded.

"And when the signal is given, get under cover, quick!"

They nodded their assent again.

"Questions?"

The groups of men had been assigned, they had their orders and their places, they knew what was expected of them. They looked at one another. Juan Three-fingers said, "I think we're ready, *Patrón*. There's just one thing. . . ."

"What's that?"

"We're horsemen. We're a tiny bit worried about how we'll do as sailors. Some of us . . . well, it's a long way from the land."

Stackpole spoke up. "I will be with you, amigos. You will do well, I know. If you throw your dinner up, do it away from the wind. This is all that is asked of you for the sailor part of things."

The vaqueros grinned and nodded, and Juan said, "Away from the wind, right?"

"*Sí*, and away from me."

~ 20 ~

THE ASSAULT

BERNARDO WAS WITH DON ALEJANDRO. They had parted into groups on the ridge. The don's group had continued along the ridge and made its way down the spine of the island to the beach. There they changed directions and crept along the beach, under cover of the dark trees, to the western edge of the slavers' valley.

Now they waited for Scar's signal that his group had reached the eastern edge of the valley. If all went well, he and his vaqueros should be in the trees across from the don's men.

A light from the trees! It went out, appeared again, went out, appeared. Three flashes of light.

Don Alejandro beckoned to Bernardo for the little lantern. He took it carefully. It was hot from the invisible candle burning inside it. He pointed it toward the location of the three flashes and opened the lantern's tiny door three times.

Two flashes came back as Scar confirmed that they were ready, and the don opened his own lantern twice. Don Alejandro had taken the longest route. When he was in place, the other groups would almost surely be ready.

"Stay behind me," he whispered to Bernardo. To his men he said, "Armbands?"

Each fingered the white armband on his left arm. If it came to a hand-to-hand fight, they would identify friends.

"Grenade," he whispered. A round clay pot packed with gunpowder and a fuse was handed up to him. It was tied to an arm's-length cord.

"Muskets, spread out and be ready. Make sure of your targets."

Half a dozen blackbirders sat around a campfire, talking and singing.

Don Alejandro opened the lantern and thrust the fuse inside. When the fuse began to hiss, he handed the lantern back to Bernardo and stepped out from the bushes. He swung the grenade around by its cord, faster and faster. The fuse sputtered and made a circle of sparks.

Bernardo could see another circle of sparks where Scar's men lay hidden.

Don Alejandro let the cord go and the grenade soared up and over the clearing. One of the slavers had time to rise, point, and say, "Look!"

The grenade exploded with a roar and a flash of light.

When the grenade from Scar's group exploded, the light caught every slaver looking up with his mouth open. This moment of light was enough for the musket men on each side of them to aim and fire. The rattle of muskets faded into the howls and screams of slavers who had been hit.

Don Alejandro shouted, "Up and at them, caballeros!" Whooping and yelling, the vaqueros picked up swords and pikes and ran up the valley. The noise from Scar's group was just as frightening.

The blackbirders' camp burst into confusion. The slavers around the fire who hadn't been hit leaped and ran uphill from the charging vaqueros. Slavers who had been asleep a moment before bolted from their tents. They met their fleeing comrades and caught their panic. Almost all the slavers ran up toward the stockade.

Don Alejandro stopped and brought up a silver whistle. It screeched in the dark. All of his men and all of Scar's men stopped their charge immediately. They all fell flat or leaped behind tree trunks. The don pushed Bernardo to the ground behind a fallen trunk and fell over him to protect the boy.

The slavers were still running. They were coming to the stockade. Behind it was safety: a thick forest where they could hide.

"Gentlemen," Regina said. She stepped out of the tree line with the retired soldiers. Two of them hefted big musketoons with bell-shaped muzzles. The others carried fowling pieces. When they could clearly see the shapes of the slavers coming up the hill, Regina gave out a bone-chilling Gabrieleño war whoop. It may have cheered several of her tribe in the stockade, but it rattled the old soldiers beside her. They fired. Each of the musketoons spat out a hundred musket balls in a blaze of orange and white fire. The fowling pieces fired ten balls each. The line of running slavers was instantly blasted to a stop.

Only a few blackbirders were untouched. These and the wounded who could run changed direction and pelted back downhill, totally confused.

Regina whooped again and pursued them, swinging her sword. The soldiers laid down their flintlocks and followed her with their own swords.

Diego and Estafina bolted out of the tree line with axes. They hurried directly to the stockade. "Stand back, brothers!" Estafina shouted. There was a stir of bodies inside the stockade and Montez called to her, but she was already attacking the stockade wall. Diego slipped around to the front of the stockade and swung his ax at the heavy lashings that made the hinge of the gate.

"Give a heave!" Diego shouted and stepped back. Several of the men inside threw themselves at the hated gate and the rope hinges parted. The gate flew open and bodies tumbled out.

"Uphill! Into the trees!" Diego shouted. "Go for the light! Don't go downhill! Uphill! Away from the beach!"

Men swarmed out of the gate and out of the broken wall. They moved toward the lantern that Trinidad had opened for them to allow the light to show.

Regina and her group gathered the surrendering slavers.

"*Patrón!*" Juan Three-fingers shouted at Don Alejandro. "Some of them are getting away!"

Slavers from one of the tents had run around Scar's group to the beach and were in a small boat, rowing frantically toward the ship anchored in the sheltered channel off the beach. In the silence that had fallen over the clearing, their oars could be heard thrashing the water. There was a chopping sound from the ship, and the sound of men running on deck.

Don Alejandro saw a square light open in the ship's side and heard a rumble. He realized with a shock what it was and what was about to happen. He blew his whistle hard. "Down!" he shouted. "Take cover! Take cover from the water side!" Again he threw Bernardo down and covered him.

A moment later there was a giant explosion, louder than the muskets and grenades together. Instantly the air was filled with whining buzzes. The slave ship had run out a cannon and fired a single round of canister. A thousand musket balls came screaming up the valley. But the only human screams came from the water. The escaping slavers were directly in the line of fire. The balls tore them and their boat to pieces.

Bernardo heard a splash beside the ship as its anchor rope was cut. He heard the squeal of ropes running through blocks, and the rustle of sails taking the wind. The slave ship swung away and gathered speed down the channel.

Its cannon couldn't aim for them at this new angle. The guerilla army ashore watched it go. They realized that they were seeing it in the first dim light of morning.

Conch-shell horns sounded as the little fleet of fishing boats rounded the eastern point, come to take their *Angeleño* friends back home.

Stackpole was first off a boat and into the water. He carried a boarding ax, a nasty-looking weapon like a large tomahawk. He surged through the water, faltering as his whalebone peg pushed into the sand but coming ahead with a murderous expression. Don Alejandro and the boys walked down to meet him.

"Trinidad?" Her safety was his first concern.

He hadn't wanted to let her go, but Regina had said, "She has a warrior's heart, Señor Stackpole. You can protect a warrior only so far. I will watch over her for her *papá*." Stackpole had never dared think of her as his daughter until that moment. He relented.

So now Don Alejandro put his hand on Stackpole's shoulder. "She is well, unharmed. We couldn't have done this thing without her. If I had a medal to give—"

Trinidad came running down the hill, leaping over a slaver's body as if it were a log. "Stackpole," she crowed, "you should have seen it! It was amazing! Shots everywhere, grenades, explosions, and the slavers tried to kill us all, but they just killed their own blackbirders!"

Stackpole's face sagged at her description. The danger! The awful possibilities!

Don Alejandro shook Stackpole's shoulder. "Don't trouble yourself, *Capitán*. I will tell you everything later. It wasn't as perilous as our Trinidad describes it. It was more like cattle in the killing chutes. Messy but businesslike."

The boys could see that Stackpole didn't believe him. He put his arm around Trinidad as she ran up, something they had never seen him do. Of course, he was a Boston man, and the emotions of that distant, rocky coast were cool.

"Now," the don said, "there are the usual details."

21

THE CONFESSION

THE BOYS WALKED AWAY with him, glad to give Stackpole some time with Trinidad. Scar fell in with them.

Don Alejandro asked, "Prisoners?"

"Only a few, *Patrón*. Two of them wounded in the first firing, three who surrendered."

"Let's have a word or two with the prisoners," he said.

All five prisoners were propped against the log that had sheltered Bernardo and Don Alejandro. The uninjured had their hands and feet bound. One wounded man was unconscious, one was gasping and crying. The don looked at their wounds, then at Scar, who shook his head: they wouldn't survive.

"Take these three to a tent. No one is to speak with

them," he ordered. Juan Three-fingers and two of his crew hefted the bound slavers over their shoulders. Diego watched them walk across to the flap of a tent and toss the slavers in, just like sacks of grain. They strode away looking as if they'd bitten into a bad apple. They had no stomach for touching men like that.

Don Alejandro squatted down beside one of the crying prisoners. "Water!" he called. He helped the man to drink. "You are dying, *hermano*. You have led a wicked life. What do you wish to tell me?"

The man gulped and whined, "I did nothing. I am a sailor. This is my only crime. I followed orders."

The don shook his head. "No, no, that will not do. You have been a thief of lives. You've taken men from their families. You've pushed them into stinking holds in chains. How many died, *hermano*? How many did you throw overboard?"

The man's eyes were frightened.

"Tell me your sins, and I will have the padre pray for you. Perhaps you may be forgiven. Perhaps if you tell me who stole the lives of the padre's men, he will grant you forgiveness."

"*Sí, Patrón.*" The man was all cooperation now.

"Tell me your sins, and I will tell the padre." He bent so his ear was at the man's lips. The lips moved rapidly, and tears streamed down the man's face, washing a path of clean skin through the filth. The don nodded and rose again. "I will speak to the padre, *hermano*, you have my word. And now tell me who told you to steal these men."

"Our captain. Captain Pew told us where to land, to pick up blackbirds, and bring them here in boats."

"But who captured them by land?"

"Hard men. Vaqueros from the south."

"And who gave orders to these hard men, *hermano*?"

"I don't know, *Patrón*. I would tell you. I swear to you on my death, I don't know."

Don Alejandro nodded. He turned to one of his vaqueros. "Make this man comfortable. Give him water; do your best." He looked down at the man again. "Perhaps a little brandy to ease the pain?"

The dying man nodded gratefully.

"See to it," the don said simply, then rose. "You have my word, *hermano*," he said, and walked toward the tent.

Diego caught up with him. "You called that slaver 'brother,' *Papá*."

The don nodded. "All dying men are brothers, Diego. It is the journey we all make."

"What will you do with these prisoners?" Diego

asked, looking toward the tent.

The don nodded his head from side to side: We shall see.

Diego suddenly had a notion of what the don would do. As they stepped past one of the slaver's bodies, Diego drew the knife from his boot and wiped blood on it from the man's wounds. He handed it to Don Alejandro.

The don took it. He kept walking, looked at the knife carefully, then said, "Sometimes, Diego, I worry that you can be too cool, too cleverly calculating. You have the ability to be ruthless. Yes, this is what I'm doing. A deception. But I want you to consider something. Your life can be cleaner, more merciful, more just than my life as a soldier. Will you think about that for me?"

"*Sí, Papá.*"

"Thank you, son. You and Bernardo stay here." He entered the tent.

The boys didn't stay, but hurried around behind the tent to listen. The don's voice was different now. It had a new edge. "Here, I have given your shipmates help to the other world." They could imagine him holding the bloody knife before the captives. "They were dying. Who knows how long they would have lasted? But you . . . with you I can be an artist. I can keep you healthy men alive for a very long time. Some of my vaqueros have great talent in keeping a man alive and screaming for days. It will take a while, and they will enjoy it. I like to give them their little pleasures."

"No, *Patrón!*"

"Oh, yes. You are now only a source of amusement for my men."

"No, we are men too!"

"Hardly. You're slavers. Not men."

"Patrón!"

"You may be of some small use to me. I might make things simpler for you."

"Whatever! Tell us! Don't let them at us!"

"Yes, you could be some source of information. For instance, the men who stole *Angeleños* ashore. Who were they?"

"Wicked dogs from the south, *Patrón!* We are simple sailors!"

The don laughed in a way the boys had never heard. It gave them chills. "I believe you will not help me after all." The boys heard his boots creak as he rose to go.

"No, *Patrón!* We will tell you anything! They were vaqueros from south of Panama. Their leader's name was Diablura. They brought the men to us on the beach."

"Did you ever see them in daylight?"

The other prisoner's voice answered, "*Sí, Patrón.* Once. We met them on the road between the pueblo and the docks."

"Think carefully now. Your lives and the way they end may depend on it. The brand on their horses' rumps, what was it?"

A silence, then spluttering as the prisoners tried to remember anything about the brand. "I don't know! I don't know brands!" one whined. "I can't remember anything for sure. All I know is that it was ornate, complicated, all swirls and lines!"

"Diego!" the don called, but the men thought he was summoning his savage vaquero torturers. They cried and wailed. Diego pushed his head through the tent flap.

"*Sí, Patrón?*" He would not call him "*Papá*" near these men.

"Across the clearing Scar has found a tent full of hides and tallow. Go cut me off a brand. You know the one."

Diego ran across the little valley, motioning for Bernardo. "Give me your knife!" he hissed. "Mine is doing its job in the tent!"

In the warehouse tents, Diego cut the lashings on a block of hides and found the brand on the top hide. He cut it free and ran back to the tent. Don Alejandro took the piece of hide and shook it under the prisoners' noses without a word.

"*Sí, sí!* That is the brand on the horses! Don't let them kill us, *Patrón!*"

Don Alejandro rose and walked out of the tent as the prisoners wailed, trying to call him back, calling on the names of God and saints. He nodded toward the tent and said to Juan, "Give them some water. They don't deserve it, but give them some anyway."

Bernardo took the hide from the don's hand and turned it over. Some of the brand was burned deeper than other parts. Bernardo traced the de la Vega *V* in the shallow burns. The don nodded. Scar spat into the sand.

Regina and Trinidad, with the vaqueros and the old soldiers, had crossed the ridge to boats drawn up on the other side of the island. The skilled men of the pueblo were wading out to the fishermen's boats. There would surely be a fiesta in the pueblo tonight.

Only Don Alejandro, Scar, Stackpole, Juan Three-fingers, Diego, and Bernardo were left on the beach. Scar nodded to the pile of slaver bodies on the sand.

"They came from the sea, let the sea take them back," Don Alejandro said. "Have the prisoners push them out into the current."

"What then for the prisoners, *Patrón?*" Scar asked. From his look, he had ideas of his own.

The don looked at Diego. "Mercy," he said. "I want you to think about mercy, Diego. Mere justice is hollow without it."

"Should we take our prisoners to the *comandante* in the pueblo?" Diego asked.

"We could, but would it be merciful? These men could be an embarrassment for Don Moncada. The *comandante* is close to the don. It might be too convenient if the prisoners met a quick and quiet accident in their cell one night. I plan to leave these men here. It's a harsh island. Perhaps they will not last out the season. They may be taken up by another ship. I will leave their fate in their own hands. Perhaps—though it is a dim possibility—they will even learn something."

"*Patrón?*" Scar asked again.

"Take anything you can find in the camp. We'll dump it at sea. Give each man a flask of water and a knife. Chance enough. They'll probably kill one another, but it's a chance."

"Moncada's hides and tallow?"

"Burn them. Moncada will never make a penny on his stolen goods, and I don't want any part of them. Burn the whole camp."

After all the excitement and noise, after the stink of gunpowder and blood, Diego didn't feel like himself. The boy who read and dreamed and played games in the comfortable hacienda was far away. He hoped he could return to being that boy. It helped, he found, to think of something purely beautiful—like Esmeralda Avila. He clung to her image now. He wondered if that was why love was important: it gave you hope that life could be fresh again.

The sun climbed, the fishing boats set sail one by one, and the line of boats sailed down the channel past the bodies of blackbirders just beginning to attract the attention of small fish.

Diego and Bernardo were in the fishing boat piloted by Stackpole, with Scar and the don.

Bernardo looked back toward the billowing black smoke from the burning hides and tallow. He nudged Diego. On the beach the three unwounded slavers were dancing up and down in a fury, making rude gestures, calling out challenges and waving the knives they'd been given.

"They seem to have a new supply of courage," Diego said. "*Capitán* Stackpole, can you do something for me?"

"Sure," Stackpole said.

"Turn the boat around for a moment and head back to the beach. Just for a moment."

Stackpole grinned and put the tiller hard over, taking in the sheet. The boat spun and headed back for the beach.

The slavers stopped leaping and stood still for a heartbeat. The boat with the guerrilla army was coming back to get them! They fled from the beach, kicking up sand with every leap.

"Thank you," Diego said.

"No, thank you," Stackpole replied, spinning the boat again to follow the others. "I wouldn't have missed that for anything."

When they reached the channel between the island and the mainland, they saw Trinidad's boat in the distance. Regina was with her. Fishing boats carried the old soldiers. All the boats were on converging courses, headed for the point above San Pedro.

Looking ahead, Stackpole grew worried. "Take the

tiller," he said to Diego. "Just hold it steady." He pulled a telescope from a canvas bag under the seat and stood up, steadying himself at the mast. "Bad luck!" he said.

"What?" Don Alejandro asked.

"The slave ship. It's run down to San Pedro ahead of us."

"What are they doing?" Diego asked.

"If I was them," Stackpole replied, "I'd be picking up the rest of my crew and any trace that they'd been there. They have hours before we can reach them."

"That means—" Diego began.

"That means the waters will be muddied," Don Alejandro said.

ᐱ 22 ᐱ

The Confrontation

A S THEY ROUNDED THE point above San Pedro, they saw the slave ship's boats rowing out to rejoin the dark ship. The boats were filled with men.

"Telescope?" Scar asked.

Stackpole handed it over, and Scar rose beside the mast. He took his time and focused, watched, then said, "Southern vaqueros, gauchos from the grasslands, by their hats and gear. We won't see them in the pueblo again."

"Gracias a Dios," Diego said. "God be thanked."

"Once they're gone, we can't prove who gave them their orders," Don Alejandro said.

"But *Papá,* we have the brands; we have the confessions of the slavers on the island!"

Don Alejandro watched the boats as they neared the slave ship. "We can't connect the slavers or these men directly to Moncada. Now Moncada will find it easy to say that the brands were changed by the men who are leaving. That the hides on the island were stolen. It will be easy to place the blame on those who are gone."

"But how can Don Moncada deny that they were riding Moncada horses?"

"He will say they were stolen horses." Don Alejandro sighed.

"But you can't believe that he is innocent!"

"Don Moncada is our villain, boys, but he has covered his tracks shrewdly. We will confront him with what we have, but remember what I told you about justice: a moving star, boys. Elusive, sometimes unreachable."

This was a more serious kind of riding.

They had saddled the horses left in San Pedro and were covering the road to the pueblo. They would send back horses for the freed prisoners, carts for the weak. But the real purpose of this ride was more sinister.

The don rode ahead of the column, Scar just behind him. His old soldiers rode in twos behind, then the vaqueros. The boys trailed them. This was a troop of soldiers, riding grimly on a mission, unspeaking and angry.

They thundered into the pueblo, slowing their horses to a walk. As Don Alejandro swung down from his mount, Padre Mendoza walked across the plaza, his old, tanned face worried. Before they left for the island, the don had told him there was to be a battle. He was searching Don Alejandro's face for some hint of the outcome.

Diego watched his father lean against his mount. His eyes were closed. He looked exhausted. In that moment the boy realized how much energy the don had given to protect the pueblo. He had been at it for years. Making Pueblo de los Angeles a fit place to live had taken so long, with so many battles. When would it end? Who would take over the task when the don grew older?

"Alejandro?" the padre asked.

The don nodded and opened his eyes. "We have them all. They are all safe. They wait for some horses and carts in San Pedro. We should tell their families."

The padre shared the don's weariness. So much struggle. But the lost had been found. His lined face split into a smile of gladness. "Yes, their families. And I will prepare a mass of thanksgiving for their return."

"And a fiesta, Padre. My men deserve a bit of fun for the night's work. But first I must deal with Miguel Moncada."

"You're certain he's behind all this?"

"*Sí*. No other."

"You have proof?"

"Every string in this web loops toward Moncada."

"Proof?"

The don shook his head. "No. We know he changed the brands of mission cattle, de la Vega cattle, probably the cattle of other ranchos. We found bales of hides and a hundred bags of tallow on the island. But no, we have not seen the don with his hand on a branding iron. All we have for his reasons are a few unguarded words by Rafael Moncada. It's possible that Señor Moncada's ambition is so overblown that he wants his own colony, somewhere across the sea. This is why our men were stolen. But no one has seen him take a man prisoner. No one but the foreign cowboys can connect him to the kidnappings. Now they are gone. We saw them board the slave ship as we sailed down the channel."

Bernardo touched Don Alejandro on the shoulder. He beckoned to the men to follow him.

The events of the night, the evil of the slavers, and the violence of the assault had sickened Bernardo. He had wanted nothing more than to be alone for a time. He had walked off the plaza and past the lines of pueblo houses, out toward the plain. He had found a strange thing there.

He stood with Diego and the men before a prickly pear cactus behind Porcana's pottery. Mounted on a prickly pear's oval branches were three hats, each stuck to the cactus with a knife.

"Gaucho hats," Scar said.

"What does this mean?" the padre asked.

Diego stepped up and fingered one of the hat brims. "These are the hats of the men who killed Señor Porcana. They are dead. You will never find them."

"Who has done this thing?"

"El Chollo," Diego replied.

They gazed at the hats. "Leave them there until they rot," Don Alejandro said. "Now for Moncada." He turned and strode toward the plaza.

The padre shook his head and called after him, "Alejandro, I fear that he has outmaneuvered you this time."

Don Alejandro turned. Diego and Bernardo couldn't believe what the padre was saying. Could Moncada escape justice? Was the star of justice this elusive?

"Yes," the padre went on. "He arrived at the pueblo

this afternoon. He says he has discovered that foreign villains have been changing brands, capturing men, and deceiving all of us."

Don Alejandro kicked a stone that rattled against a wall. It was a rare show of temper.

"What is his proof?" the don said after a time.

"A dead vaquero over a saddle. He says the man confessed everything before he died. He accused a cowboy named Diablura and a slaver captain named Pew. Moncada insists that these are the guilty men."

"Do you believe him?" Don Alejandro asked.

"I examined the dead vaquero. I can't prove it, but I believe he was strangled before he was shot. He was the scapegoat. They needed someone."

The don looked out over the plain. "Well, old friend, we have played chess enough to recognize that some games must be stalemates."

"We can't let him get away with this!" Diego blurted. Bernardo moved up close beside him.

Don Alejandro smiled without humor. "He has saved his skin. For now. But we know that he is a danger to this pueblo. To all of us." A remarkable change came over the don. "Come. Let us congratulate Don Miguel Moncada for solving this mystery."

Scar spat.

♦ ♦ ♦

"Wine! Wine for our brave captain!" Moncada called. He was seated at a table beneath the inn's trellis. "I am told you have beaten the slavers and rescued all of our pueblo's men!"

"All but one. Señor Porcana. A brave little man who fought and showed us the way."

"You are the soul of courage. The blood of El Cid, that great warrior hero, runs in your Spanish blood, Don Alejandro. We have so much to thank you for."

The boys couldn't believe their ears. The don bowed deeply in appreciation of these compliments, sat, and accepted the glass of wine. How could he bear to sit with this vile man?

"The credit goes to my vaqueros and to my old soldiers, Don Miguel. I am certain you will want to reward them in some splendid way for returning the pueblo to rights."

With only a heartbeat of pause, Moncada cried, "Of course! I will shower them with gold and horses! And you, *Capitán*?"

"My reward is your good opinion of me, Don Miguel. I am content."

"But name anything! What can I do for you?"

"There is one small thing, señor. Your brand, the iron

221

poppy. So beautiful, yet we have seen it is easy to change. Perhaps a simpler, less changeable brand?"

"I will have the blacksmith at work in the morning on a new brand for the Moncada cattle and horses!"

"Admirable speed, but anytime soon would be wise. And practical. If our vaqueros saw more changed brands, tempers might grow thin in the pueblo. A simple brand shouldn't set us apart. Are we not all settlers in this new land together?"

"All of us together, here on the edge of the Spanish world!" Moncada lifted his glass.

"Spanish? Yes, it is our heritage. But, my dear don, we are really *Californios*. This is a new land. Rougher, stronger. The delicate judgments of the Spanish courts are far away. Here, the distinctions between right and wrong aren't made in the courts, but in the saddle. Scheming men would do well to consider our rough justice."

A moment of doubt flickered across Moncada's face. To hide it, he set his face in a mask of righteous anger. "I have such a man on a packhorse outside. He was part of the band of villains who deceived all of us."

"Was he, then? *Está bien.* It's good that evil men have been exposed," Don Alejandro said. He lifted his glass to Moncada and looked him in the eye for so long that

Moncada's gaze faltered, his eyes shifted away. Don Alejandro touched the rim of Moncada's glass, forcing his eyes back. "I think we understand each other, Don Miguel. *Salud.*"

They drank the pueblo's wine. Moncada looked away again. Bernardo touched Diego's back. Diego nodded. They had just heard Don Alejandro make a dangerous challenge, voiced in the elaborate politeness of hidalgo courtesy.

"Come, my boys. We have someone to thank."

"Who, *Papá*?"

"Señora Porcana, for the courage of her husband. Then we have a long ride to the de la Vega hacienda. Estafina will get there before we do. She'll have a good dinner waiting."

They walked along the streets of their pueblo.

"*Papá* . . . ," Diego began, then faltered. He was so frustrated he couldn't speak. Right and wrong were slipping away! Evil was going unpunished! The weak of the pueblo had been the prey of the powerful. Was there no way to make it right?

Bernardo was just as upset in his own way. He withdrew even more into himself.

"I'll try to say this plainly," Don Alejandro said,

measuring his words. "A part of me—the young blade who is still inside every old soldier—wants to walk back to the inn and skewer Moncada on my sword. I despise the man and his schemes. I despise him for a bigot and a cheat. He deserves the point of my sword."

They walked on for a time as he gathered his thoughts. "But the pueblo and my family deserve more than that. If I took it on myself to judge and execute Miguel Moncada, I would rob all of us of what is most precious: justice. We need justice by law. It must be justice not of men's passions, but of their minds, justice that is logical and civilized."

He bent to pluck one of the golden poppies from a patch of shaded grass. "So the old soldier in me quiets that young blade. The old soldier tells him that we have fought and worked these many years for a reason." He held the poppy up. "The California poppy, so bright and hopeful. This is a new land, boys. This is what we've fought for. We need courts and judges and juries—real law. Right now we have corrupt soldiers and at least one thieving hidalgo. But the land grows strong, and real justice will come. We can't shame California by going back to the old rule of might and revenge, not even if we must let someone like Moncada escape punishment."

The don could see that the boys were close to frustrated tears. He put his arms around their shoulders. "Let it go, my sons. Let it go. Satisfy yourselves with this one thing: you did your very best. You were brave and intelligent and you sought justice. Today that is enough. Tomorrow you will be men, and you can seek further justice. Now, this day, I am proud of you both."

᪁ 23 ᪁

"HASTA LUEGO"

THE *TWO BROTHERS* HAD ARRIVED. It was docked by the *Santa Inés*, a packet schooner headed for Panama.

Don Alejandro had decided to ship his hides and tallow from the docks in the daylight. He would openly defy the laws against trading through foreign vessels. If Mexico City wanted to enforce the laws, let them send regular ships. He would not allow the pueblo to suffer for Spanish neglect.

So Stackpole was stumping about, overseeing the loading of hide stacks and tallow bags. He and Captain Carter barked happily back and forth in their odd Boston English.

The boys were so fascinated by the process of hoisting and stowing that they were trying to help, mostly

226

getting in the way.

Captain Carter was not a patient soul. He loosed a stream of English at Stackpole that sounded blasphemous and was certainly directed at the boys.

Stackpole translated, probably with less than absolute accuracy. "The captain suggests that you have inspected the hold of his vessel, his crew's abilities, and most of the deck equipment. He asks if you would care to inspect the upper rigging, as a change."

It sounded like a wonderful idea. A few minutes later, the boys were perched near the top of the mainmast with a thrilling view. Naturally they had brought a few oranges—some to eat and some to drop on the heads of crew members foolish enough to stand in one place for any length of time. So far the crew had moved about steadily, but they had hopes that one tired-looking sailor would soon take a rest.

Bernardo pointed down the beach. Montez and one of the padre's carpenters were rebuilding Trinidad's shack into something more substantial and weatherproof. Regina and Trinidad were wrestling a chest of drawers through the front door. Just starting down the beach toward them, Estafina was almost hidden from above by a hide-covered chair carried on her head.

"The Trinidad Somoza hacienda," Diego said.

Bernardo made the sign for tea.

"My, yes. It's an elegant mansion. I doubt if we're fancy enough to be invited for tea. With molasses."

Regina and Trinidad came out and sat on the new front porch, waiting for Estafina and the chair.

"Look at them, chatting like magpies."

Bernardo frowned, then looked at Diego with a question in his brows.

"I'm afraid so," Diego replied. "Apparently we have a sister."

Diego wondered how Esmeralda and Trinidad would react to each other. They seemed so different, but he had been wrong about Trinidad and Regina, hadn't he?

Bernardo pointed to a trail of dust along the road to the pueblo.

"I suppose that will be King Pompous and Prince Dandy." Diego felt the Moncadas deserved royal titles if they were planning to have their own kingdom. A cart had arrived earlier with two dozen pieces of Rafael Moncada's baggage. He was leaving for Barcelona and the university.

Bernardo signed to Diego: Maybe he will throw up on the ship.

"Good thought! We can hope he is seasick all the

way to Barcelona. He might even catch some grim fever in Panama. That would save the university the trouble of trying to push lessons into his thick head."

They watched the Moncadas ride up to the dock. Father and son were dressed in white brocade with blue sashes. Silver glinted from their saddles.

"Very showy. A lot of extra weight for the horses to carry."

Bernardo nodded.

"We should make our good-byes."

The boys forgot their hopes of orange dropping and climbed down to the deck. They walked back along the dock to the *Santa Inés*.

Rafael's baggage was stowed. The last of the water barrels had been rolled aboard the schooner's deck. Miguel Moncada, who would accompany his son to Panama, was speaking with the schooner's captain in his cabin.

"What schemes does King Pompous have in Panama? I can't believe he's making the trip just because he loves Prince Dandy. Well, I suppose even skunks love their babies," Diego conceded.

Don Moncada came on deck and stood at the stern. He waved with charming guile to the boys and they waved back. Beside him, the captain gave orders to cast off the schooner's lines and make sail.

Rafael came up a ladder onto the deck. He saw Diego and Bernardo standing on the dock and swaggered over to the rail in his white finery.

"So you've come to see me off to Barcelona, little boys. I'm off to the university and the fencing schools."

Diego bowed. "We've come to wish you a happy arrival in Barcelona. We hope you will be very content there."

"Insincere wishes from half-breeds do not interest me," Rafael said.

"But we're sincere in these wishes, Rafael," Diego assured him. "We hope you delight in Barcelona's many beauties. We trust you will like it so much that you will make your home there. Consider that California is dirty and not at all elegant. It's not a proper place for you. We think you should stay in Spain. I can just see you reveling in the wealth of your aunt Eulalia, making friends with the courtiers. Can't you see him there, Bernardo? Your style should fit perfectly. I should think you'd find our humble pueblo terribly boring after life in that lively city. It would be more pleasant and perhaps even healthier for you."

"Do you dare to threaten a Moncada?"

"That would be clumsy and impolite. No, let us

simply say that we know."

"Know what?"

Diego nodded to Bernardo, who threw something across the widening gap between the dock and the schooner's deck. Rafael picked it up.

"A hat with a hole and a scrap of hide. What foolishness is this?"

"The hat belonged to a bandit vaquero from the south, a slaver in your father's pay. He kidnapped men from the pueblo as slaves for the strange fantasy of a Moncada kingdom. The caballero who wore the hat is, alas, deceased. We found it pinned to a cactus with a dagger."

Moncada's mouth opened and closed. He was not a skillful liar and no good at hiding his surprise. His reaction told the boys that Rafael shared his father's secrets.

"The hide has a brand. You see? It was the brand of the iron poppy. But that is being changed to a simpler brand. The reason? Because your foreign cowboys changed other ranchos' brands and even the mission's brand to the iron poppy. Why? To finance your ridiculous Moncada colony. Yes, we know, Rafael."

"If I were on that dock I'd—" Rafael puffed himself up, trying to look threatening.

"You would do nothing. Not without a gang of

toughs around you. Stay in Spain, Rafael. We hear it's a lovely place. If you return, you will not prosper. You will have too many enemies."

"You, de la Vega, and you, you Indian idiot," Rafael spluttered, "you have made a powerful enemy. I will not rest until I destroy you. *¡Contra viento y marea!*" Come wind or water! He stood clutching the hat and hide, then stumbled as the sails took the wind and the schooner heeled. *"¡Hasta luego!"* he shouted. Until we meet again.

The distance between them widened. Rafael was so angry his family's secrets had been so thoroughly exposed that he couldn't say another word. He clutched the schooner's rail and stared at them in fury like a trapped coyote.

Diego and Bernardo waved politely to Rafael Moncada and then to his father. They turned and walked toward the *Two Brothers*.

"That was a strange good-bye," Stackpole said. "I doubt that young Moncada will send you sweet notes from Barcelona." He grinned and returned to his shouting and swearing direction of the loading.

"Diego! Bernie! You've got to see my house! It's spectacular. I have a bed and a bureau and a chair and a mirror. A big mirror. I look great in that mirror!

Montez and Chulio are putting in a window, with real glass! I have a porch and a bench to watch the sunset. You've got to see it!"

Regina caught up with her. "We have much to do before we invite visitors, little sister. Perhaps the boys can inspect it later. But now, *hijos*, the don needs your help. A rider has come. There is some strange business at the tar pits. Your father asks that you look into it."

"*Sí, Mamá.* We are at his service and on our way. *Con su permiso*, señora, señorita." With your permission, madam, miss. They bowed and backed away a few steps. Then they turned and ran to their tethered horses.

They saddled up as carefully as Scar had taught them, mounted up, and rode inland. They didn't even look back to watch the schooner's sails grow smaller. They were eager to put Rafael and his father behind them. Some new adventure was waiting for them at the tar pits. What mystery did those sticky, smelly, mysterious black pits offer today?

They rode together in the sun. Before them rolled the foothills and beyond them the mountains. The wind was behind them carrying the scent of new blooms. Why would anyone live anyplace but the golden hills of California?